THIS TOWN DIED WITH YOU

A.J. Spencer

ISBN-13: 9798825054513

Cover design by:Jenaniper
www.Jenaniper.com
Library of Congress Control Number: 2018675309
Printed in the United States of America

I'm gonna dedicate this book to Wes Craven, Don Coscarelli, Sam Raimi, and Shirley Jackson.

Thank you for the nightmares.

CHAPTER ONE

Justin lay in the darkness of his hangover-induced grave. He didn't think his phone would get reception on the way down to Hell, but the screen lit up, and when he hit the answer button, the reception was loud and clear.

"Hello?" He said weakly.

"Justin Adler! Welcome to your eternal damnation; prepare to surrender your soul to us!" Growled the voice on the other end.

"Oh, too bad, man, I don't think I have a soul anymore; I'm pretty sure I puked it up last night with all the drugs and alcohol."

"Fool!" The demon barked, "You will pay for all your sins and reckless behavior. We will fillet your flesh and feast on it using your blood as a fine dipping sauce. Then when there is nothing left, we will restore you whole and start over again!"

"Well, that sounds like a lot of fun and everything, but what I think I'll do instead is find out who this is when I sober up and beat the shit out of you," Justin snarked.

He was starting to come too, the worst headache he's ever experienced, and the agitation was pounding away at his head. He knew it was probably Trent getting one of his frat boys to prank call him, and he wanted to make it clear that he was having none of it. He felt victorious now that there was a lingering silence on the other end.

Then there was laughter, sinister, inhuman laughter. Justin wished on everything that this was a fever dream. He wasn't ready to be dead just yet. He saved his money. He would get into that school out west and study video game design if he could just wake up, but the laughter he was hearing was all too real. He couldn't let this be it. In the town where he had been trapped his entire life, he wasn't about to be devoured by some otherworldly entity.

"Oh, Justin," the demon said through his laughter. "Don't play tough; I can smell your fear; I can feel your blood turn cold. Don't fight your fate, just accept it."

Those words made Justin feel weighed down to the bed that had been his coffin for the past two days, crippled with fear. His sweat was so heavy against his scrawny body that he felt lighter with every drop that hit his sheets. Now, this felt real. The demon wasn't on the phone anymore. It was right beside him. Its breath filled the entire room with a hot desert wind.

He wasn't going out without a fight. He stealthily moved his hand between his bedside table and the wall where there was barely enough room to conceal his wooden baseball bat. The only gift his dad had ever given him. He taught Justin that going into the woods and smashing things was a great way to blow off steam. The Louisville Slugger was the only thing that made him feel safe and sane. He gripped it as hard as he could and prepared to take his best swing.

The creature was so close now that he could feel its leathery skin brush up against him. He waited until its clawed fingers reached his neck to summon his caveman instincts and swung the weapon. His eyes were closed, and he was expecting to miss, then hear the creature laugh at him again. He was shocked when the contact seemed to cause the beast pain. He felt the satisfying impact of the wood bouncing off of the demon's solid structure, followed by a very human "OUFH" sound.

"Ouch, man!" The demon squealed in a voice that was not demon-like at all and, in fact, very familiar to Justin. "I think you broke my collar bone, dude," the demon moaned. The voice was very human and even more familiar now. Justin realized he knew who it was.

He jumped to his feet and flipped the light switch on—the room filled with a light that made Justin's hangover headache go into overdrive. Next to his bed, curled up in a fetal position, was the confirmation of what he had already started to piece together.

It was his best friend, Angus Malcolm.

"Even If I still drank, I don't think there would be enough alcohol here to numb me," Angus groaned.

Next to him was a prop from a drug store. He remembered Angus talking about buying all week. A highly detailed grotesque bust of a vampire halfway through transforming into a bat. Complete with long, veiny ears, a wrinkled face with a flat nose, and long piercing fangs.

"What were you thinking?" Justin asked. He held his hand to pull his chubby friend up despite his level of aggravation. However, he should have come to expect this behavior from the guy that was known by everyone as the biggest man-child in town. He started to feel bad about whacking him with the ball bat.

"You picked the worst time to scare me," Justin said, trying to justify his behavior before Angus could make him feel guilty.

"Dude, it's almost dark. They said you've been up here passed out all day. I thought you would at least be half-awake by now and not that gullible," Angus quipped back.

Justin went to the mini-fridge he bought to avoid using the one downstairs and having his food getting stolen. He found a bag of frozen steamed vegetables, then tossed them in Angus's direction.

"Catch asshole," he said, trying to lighten the mood.

"Thanks, " Angus said sarcastically.

He was letting Justin know that his half-hearted apology wasn't good enough.

"You know, if you would have hit me a little harder, you might have made me deformed, and I wouldn't need a costume to play a monster," Angus continued.

"What are you talking about?" Justin asked.

A huge smile spread across Angus's face.

"Guess what I did." He said

Justin searched through his hazy memory. Angus had a lot of passion projects. He remembered the time Angus wanted to purchase a bunch of broke down buses and tried to live in them off the grid. Or when he tried to open up an aquarium that was also a concert venue. The thing on the floor staring at him with its glowing red eyes and blood-sucking fangs jogged his memory.

"Your opening a haunted house." He said.

Just when he thought Angus couldn't smile any wider, he did. It also made him realize just how much sobriety made Angus gain weight.

" Yup, you'll never believe how cheap I got it for either," Angus said

"How cheap, and where?" Justin asked.

He hoped Angus hadn't gotten himself into a bad deal. He was notorious for screwing himself over and owing tons of money.

"For free!" Angus exclaimed, throwing his hands up in the air. His smile faded when he realized Justin wasn't matching his enthusiasm.

"I swear, dude, you know that old crematorium that's been sitting around for the past few years on the backside of where all those hippies moved in? I was walking by it today eating a burrito and ran into the owner. For some odd reason, he looked distressed. His eyes were wild. He was super spooked. Anyways I asked him if he ever planned on selling the place. He just told me that if I cleaned the place, restored it myself, and became the primary caretaker, I could have it! You can't tell me that's not awesome."

He saw Justin consider the scenario and nod his head.

"Ok, but there's gotta be a catch; I mean, you gotta clean the place up. Who knows what's in there?" Justin said

"I'm going to open up a haunted house. I'll leave most of the stuff there to keep it spooky, duh, man." Angus rolled his eyes in response.

"Alright, but you've never run any kind of business. You think you're cut out for this?" Justin asked.

"Positive," Angus said with a thumbs up. "That's also the reason I came over here, though."

"I knew it," Justin said.

"Oh, come on. I need you to come over there with me tonight to get the keys and check the place out. I think you owe me now after you almost broke my collar bone." Angus said.

Justin huffed and rubbed his eyes. "Alright, man, but we gotta stop so I can get a sports drink or something. I need electrolytes if we're gonna be out all night."

Angus agreed, a smug grin crossing his face; that was easier than he had thought. Justin picked whatever clothes were the cleanest on the floor before they headed out. This could be the perfect opportunity for Justin to tell him that he needed a change of scenery if he was going to get his shit together and find some direction in life. He was proud of his friend, and he knew Angus wanted the same for him, but his method was different. Justin didn't want to go to the meetings at the Church-With-No-Name. He needed to leave, and he needed to get out of the party house where his frat boy roommate threw ragers all day, every day. The music was thumping through the floor as he put his shoes on, and Justin could feel his headache trying to crack his skull open. He was glad to get out of this place tonight.

CHAPTER TWO

A group of party-goers had crowded the bottom of the stairs, blocking the only exit. Justin and Angus stopped midway down, just as a chant began.

"Hit the lights! Hit the lights! Hit the Lights!" Cried the group of college kids. Most of them were way younger than Justin, making him feel more embarrassed about living with Trent. Speaking of whom was the subject of attention as always. The lights flipped off, and the room became a sea of neon glow sticks and lights from cellphone screens. In the center of the room, Trent Harper stood on a chair, shirtless aside from a scarf around his neck. His long dark hair was pulled back in a ponytail and illuminated in blue and white.

This signified that he was at his peak level, wasted, and most likely about to do something stupid. Everyone waved their glow sticks and cheered as he made his shot glass appear in one hand and a lighter in the other like he was putting on a magic trick. He flicked the lighter above the shot glass and ignited the liquor inside.

"Tonight, we drink this whole fucking city under the table!" Trent shouted.

He downed the flaming shot. The cheers got louder. Everyone simultaneously took their shot or drank from their cup or flask. Someone poured more liquor into Trent's glass while another offered him a pizza box like they were presenting it to a king. He took a piece, poured the liquor over it, and sparked another flame from the lighter. Just when it seemed like Trent wouldn't do anything dumber than his usual shenanigans, he lit the pizza on fire and showed it to his crowd of spectators. They chanted his name as he slowly brought the burning slice to his mouth. He stuck his tongue out and flicked it along the edge of the cheese that was hanging off of the edge.

Trent was always acting like a douche. Justin only roomed with him for the cheap rent and frequent party favors. He wasn't into the raging parties that seemed to happen every other night of the week. He looked at Angus, and they both shook their heads. Angus motioned for them to push their way through the crowd. They didn't want to see any more of Trent's display of chest-pounding, but before they were out the door, they got to witness the most incredible sight either of them had ever seen.

Someone in the crowd behind Trent moved quick enough to pull the chair out from underneath him without being seen. Trent fell face-first into the table where the pizza in the box sat. The thunk of his hollow skull was louder than the dubstep blaring from the speakers. He howled and rolled around on the ground while one of his so-called friends took his favorite leather jacket off the hook and threw it over him, then proceeded to pour cold beer on his head to clean him off. The sound sounds of Trent's screams grew louder when someone cut the music off. After fighting to get back on his feet, Trent used the now ruined jacket to keep his cheese and pepperoni face covered. Then he proceeded to tell everyone to leave before slamming the bathroom door shut and locking it.

No one could keep their composure, and everyone went quiet for a few seconds before they left the house, laughing hysterically at Trent and his hurt pride. Justin and Angus were the last to exit. Angus tapped Justin on the shoulder and said, "Over there!" Moving ahead of them in the crowd was a tall, brawny guy in a black muscle shirt and aviator hat. His face was covered in tattoos.

"I swear for a second that I saw that hat back there. That's the guy that made Trent fall!"

Angus quickly pursued the guy in the aviator cap. Justin followed them across the front lawn, where Angus had his rust bucket parked. A six-thousand-dollar 1994 Chevy Astro van with mismatched doors, dark blue against the silver body. Some spots had been excessively spray-painted over, causing bubbles to form. It was the only vehicle Angus had ever owned. It was also where he had been living since his accident. While working at a music venue one night, someone left a beer on top of a guitar amp, and it fell off while Angus was plugging it in, electrocuting him. It left him permanently messed up in the head. His hairstyle was wild, and always looked like he was still being fried. After that, Angus frequently wanted to have Justin drive around with him with no destination, just to clear his mind and see how long the big metal beast would make it. When they finally did break down, they had a bottle of whiskey that they would split and reflect on everything going on in their lives. They called these trips therapy sessions. Justin missed them even more now that he was drinking alone.

Angus had caught up to the aviator hat and was talking to him by the curb. As Justin approached, he caught the tail end of the conversation. Under the street light, he could make out the guy's face tattoos. One was a guitar pick on his left cheek with an evil eye etched into it and devil horns peering out from the top. Then there was a smiley face with angry eyebrows and two stick-figure arms throwing up the middle finger on each hand on his right cheek. The rest looked like tiny musical notes above his eyes and beside his ears.

"I crash parties like this all the time. I cause problems with frats because idiots like that one in there need to be put in his place. People like him think they rule the world, but on the inside, we're all just a bunch of nerds trying to find a place that we belong." The guy was saying to Angus.

"Oh yeah, I hear you; I'm glad you broke up the circus of frat bros. I was wondering if you wanted to come to hang out with my friend and me tonight. We are gonna check out this abandoned cemetery that I run now." Angus told him.

The guy considered it for a moment, then nodded.

"Sure. It's not like I have anything else going on right now."

"Hell yeah, man!" Angus exclaimed. He now noticed Justin had joined them.

"Justin, this is Neil; he's gonna ride with us. This is gonna be fun!"

Neil greeted Justin with a fist bump before getting in the trash heap with a motor. The empty burger joint and gas station food wrappers created an obstacle. The empty energy drink cans that crunched under their feet indicated that Angus still had an addiction. One that was only slightly more safe than his last one. The familiar smell of the car and the night air were already helping with the whiskey glass haze that Justin's mind was floating around in. Maybe just being heathens loose in the night like old times was part of his healing process. He needed a night away from the bright lights and thumping bass and the smell of yeast-fermented malt.

They drove off, and Justin noticed as they passed that not everyone from their townhouse had made it to a vehicle. Some opted to pass out in the yard, scattered about like the remaining corpses of an army that lost a war. Most of them snuggled up to empty bottles like security blankets. Justin wondered how many nights that had been him—only sprouting up in the morning like a drunken flower. Then he would stumble into the shower and think of reasons he should call into work, but knowing he wouldn't because he needed money. Rinse and repeat. He worked at a smoke shop called Sunny Blaze, selling "tobacco products." He was a natural who looked perfect for the job since he was tall, skinny, and unshaven. Also, he was able to come to work dressed in his favorite red flannel pajama pants, band t-shirts, and a black beanie to cover up his balding head, which was, of course, his current attire. Having no dress code was love. So was the laid-back environment and shooting the shit with his fellow smokers all day. He didn't mind it, but sometimes it would get boring, and all he would have to think about was how his life hit a dead end. It wasn't a career, and he would never save up any money. One day he was getting the mail for his manager. He spotted a pamphlet for a school for video game design in California near Venice beach. Something about that called to him, and he looked into it several times.

There had to be a way to get out of this cycle and claw his way there. If only he could talk Angus into coming with him, but why would he? This place had always been a part of Angus, he would never leave, and now he had acquired a piece of its history.

CHAPTER THREE

Hippie Street was a long strip of the town painted with bright murals that said things like "Heaven Is Here On Earth!". Usually right above a depiction of a globe with angel wings. This was meant to show how progressive the dive bars were. In reality, it just became a place for college kids to pose for selfies to post on their multiple social media accounts. It was one thing Justin hated about what the city was becoming. Soon it would be all trendy bars and restaurants. The driving service Ready to Ride always had the road clogged with their vehicles slowing down traffic to a crawl. Neil had the auxiliary cord hooked into his phone, and the sounds of fast percussive beats and low register guitar riffs filled up the car with aggressive energy. When Neil noticed that Justin and Angus were nodding their heads and enjoying the vibe, he smiled and told them, "You like this? It's my old band." In his most proud tone.

"You guys don't play anymore? This makes me wanna punch my stepdad. I love it," Angus said.

"What were you guys called?" Justin asked.

"We were called Iron Burial," Neil said unenthusiastically. "Not my first pick. We recorded this whole thing in an old utility closet at my friend's house. I still can't believe it sounds this good."

"Dude, that name is perfect for this attraction I'm starting up! You see, I bought one of the last relics in this whole city. I'm gonna turn it into a haunted attraction during Halloween. Before opening night at the haunted house, you have to come shred. Well, set up a stage in the crematorium and everything!" Angus said.

"It's been a while since I've picked up my ax. I might be rusty; lately, I've just been busy trying to keep my lights on and watching all my dreams die, ya know?" Neil said. His voice started to shake on the last sentence as if he had never said it out loud before, and hearing it made it have more emotional weight.

The traffic finally began to move, much to the excitement of the drunk party kids in their rideshare vehicles. Some of them shouted slurred cries of joy and howled like wolves when the cars moved. They continued through Hippie Street and reached the section least lit by streetlights and less populated with trendy hangouts. This was still a poor neighborhood. It was known to the locals as Ash Land. Promptly named because its most prominent building was the one they were about to arrive at. They could see it getting closer, growing in size, and coming into focus as if being looked at through a telescopic lens. The rectangular building with the shadow of the smokestack sticking up was beckoning them to come closer, just a little closer. Then they were there parked in front of it. The moonlight highlighted the monotone graffiti. Graffiti was hideous and vulgar, unlike the bright and colorful images found on Hippie Street. A severed head with an expressionless face and two Xs for eyes greeted visitors at the front. Positive messages were replaced with 666 written in various sizes, and a pentagram with a mouth in the center screamed at them.

"Well, you gotta admire that kind of dedication," Angus said, pointing to a giant penis shooting fire out of the tip that was spray painted the entire length of one side of the building.

"I think you have more work ahead of you than you thought," Justin added.

"Doesn't get more welcoming than that," Neil said.

Angus took out his phone and tried to call Lester as they crossed the cemetery gates and approached the building. He hung up, tried one more time, then another. By this time, they were standing outside the large entrance to the crematorium. The two large wooden doors were further secured by a metal gate that was locked uptight.

"Oh come on, don't tell me that bastard lied to me," Angus cried out. He tried rattling the gate, but it held tight. Justin was about to tell him to call the whole thing off before he went off toward the back of the building toward the cemetery.

"Lester! Are you here, you old bastard?" He called out at the top of his lungs.

Justin and Neil followed. The trees were as dead as the people resting in the ground. They shook with the night wind, blowing the overgrown grass across the trios' legs. When the grass parted, hidden grave sites could be seen peaking through. Angus had given up on his shouting and threw his hands up in defeat.

"I can't believe this," he said. They looked around at the empty graveyard. It looked like it hadn't been cared for in years. Headstones were full of cracks. Headless statues still held out praying hands, and some of the family crypts were missing bricks. Instead, they were lazily filled in with misshapen objects.

"Look at this place, Angus. Take this as a sign; this place is way beyond repair," Justin said.

"Nah, man, I had a vision for this place. I was so close to marking this one off my list. I can't just leave and regret it forever. The old man said he'd be here. He's gotta be here somewhere." Angus replied.

"Maybe he went in there," Neil added

At the back of the building was a concrete ramp that led down to another large iron door. The wind pulled it open, and the screeching hinges called out to them before slamming it shut again.

"Maybe you should call him again before we go in there. Especially if that's what I think it is," Justin said.

"Oh yeah, that's definitely where they used to cart bodies in," Neil said.

" Then we are going in there," Angus said

The two were already heading into the dark entrance before Justin could protest. He hesitated until he realized he was standing alone, then followed the sound of their voices. The concrete walls seemed to get more and more narrow as they fumbled through and found their phones.

"Tell me again why we didn't bring a flashlight?" Justin asked.

Neither one answered as they turned on the flashlights on their cellphones. Revealing the concrete ramp, they headed down. The walls were covered in more graffiti. " BURN WITH US" in all capital letters, dripped in bright red and yellow paint. Everything else mostly consisted of occult symbols that Neil informed them were wrong and told them that satanic posers must have had been there. They are probably doing fake rituals that they downloaded off of Reddit. It was edgy to be in a cult nowadays. Then they finally entered the lower level of the building and found the room where the bodies were put in the incinerators. In the middle of the sizeable square-shaped room were two oversized metal furnaces. The paint had chipped off them, and their control panels had their cover torn off. Leaving exposed wire peering out.

"Feeling inspired to write a song yet, Neil?" Angus asked.

" Maybe, This is pretty wicked," Neil responded.

This is good, Justin thought. He's making a new friend and won't even miss me when I'm out. A sudden popping sound made him jump, and the flickering of fluorescent bulbs filled the room with a dull light.

"Found the switch," Said Angus

" Ha! Check this out." Neil chuckled.

He pointed out that someone had written: "45 seconds for a frozen pizza" on the side of one of the machines. They laughed, but Justin noticed one difference between the two machines that made him uneasy. The door to the one with the frozen pizza instructions was still closed and locked. Immediately he pictured someone's remains still trapped in there, burned, but not all the way to completely make the body disappear. Just a charred and unrecognizable lump. Like a frozen pizza someone forgot to take out of the oven.

"So, you're gonna make this place safe for people to walk through?" Justin asked.

He looked around at the debris all over the floor where the building had begun to fall apart. Doors to the storage rooms had dropped off and lay on the floor, a broken office chair was bent backward at the top, and the rip in the cushion made it look like it was tilting its head back and laughing maniacally. Behind it in the exposed storage closet were long forgotten tombstones.

"Are you kidding me?" Angus said, rushing past him to get a look at the cracked markers. "This place barely needs to be touched in time for haunt season. Look at all these props we already have. All we need now are some flashing lights, a fog machine, props, and sound effects."

As if right on cue, they heard the sounds of footsteps from above them. Coming from the upper floor.

"Sounds like the old man is in here for sure," Angus said.

"What's on the upper part anyway?" Neil asked.

"We are about to find out," Angus told him.

CHAPTER FOUR

The stairs leading to the upper floor were the worst part of the structure. Each time the trio took another step, the wood let out a groan that echoed throughout the narrow passageway. In between groans were the sounds of excited whispers.

"Let's hurry up and shoot this. We aren't supposed to be in here."

Said one voice that was younger, feminine, and not Lester.

"I know, but look at all these papers scattered all over the floor. These records go back to the 1800s, and can you believe that door was just open!?"

Said another voice, much like the first one.

"Of course, the door was open; this place was begging for a cleansing."

Said a third voice.

The trio on the stairs stopped to look at each other, each wondering what they were about to walk into. Justin took another step and gave them away with the loudest creak.

"Oh hell, someone's coming. What do we do now?" One of the voices asked.

"Just be cool; the worst they'll do is make us leave. At least we still have the footage from the Cemetery. Quick, put the camera away!"

The guys reached the top of the steps and entered a church-type cathedral where three girls were standing in the center of the large candlelit room.

Two were dressed in all dark black attire. One was a tall black girl with a short pixie hair cut, a pale-skinned girl tall with blue streaks throughout blonde, and one shorter girl with long, wavy brown hair and fierce blue eyes. That other one looked nothing like the other two. She was dressed in a simple bright green tee shirt and jeans. Her thick-rimmed glasses gave her more of a female professor look than the satanic look; in her hand was a phone decked out with professional recording gear, including a small boom mic and a studio light.

"Cut," said the camera girl upon seeing the three guys enter. The phone made a loud beeping sound as she shut it off. The blonde rolled her eyes as the short-haired one broke the ice.

"Hey, I'm gonna take a wild guess and say that you three aren't supposed to be here anymore than we are, and as you can see, we are trying to work on something here."

"Yeah, looks like some cult shit to me." Said Angus.

"Oh, is that what it looks like?" Said the short-haired witch, visibly offended.

Angus shrugged and gestured vaguely to the candles and the girls' outfits.

"The candles are actually for getting rid of evil; for your information, we are about to burn some sage too. The cloaks we are wearing are traditional. We are cleansing this place. Mediums and demonologists aren't Satanists!" She added.

"Ok, my fault," Angus said, throwing his hands up in defense.

"For the record, I think this magic shit is pretty cool," Neil added.

"Sierra, we aren't going to be able to finish this now. Let's just go." the blonde-haired girl said.

"No!" said Sierra. "They intruded in on us. We were here first."

"Well, I hate to break it to you, but I kind of run this whole place now. You're looking at the new caretaker." Angus told her.

Sierra rolled her eyes and called a huddle with her crew. Angus did the same with his.

"Can you believe this shit? They are trying to ruin our whole thing." He said.

"Yeah, but they're kind of hot. You don't think we should ask them to hang with us?" Neil asked.

"Maybe talk to them like a civilized adult and not be a jerk; people tend to respond to you better if you're not like that," Justin added.

He knew that if they didn't resolve this situation, this experience would be drawn out even longer. Then he'd never see the "You are now leaving" sign as he drove away from this hell hole. Although the one named Sierra, something about her caught his eyes. He couldn't help but stare at her over Angus's shoulder, whose argument was going in one ear and out the other. He and Neil already had him out voted anyways. Sierra whipped around and, for a second, made direct eye contact. He knew that this night was supposed to be a hangout for mainly he and Angus, but he really wouldn't mind if they stuck around.

Now they were coming this way. Justin decided to be diplomatic and help them reach a compromise.

"Ok, let us make a deal." Sierra said, "you let us film our video, and we'll let you be a part of it. We will interview you and let you give us a tour and everything. Then people will know who you are and pay you good money to see this, um, landmark."

Angus looked to Justin and Neil, both of who nodded heavily in agreement.

"Fine." He said, "Then as soon as we're done, you out of here?"

"Scouts honor." All three girls said while holding up their right hands

"Well then, let us do this," Angus said

The blonde, whose name turned out to be Katherine, went ahead of them to find out where the most paranormal activity would likely be. Danielle, the camera girl, did her best to make Angus look more professional. She tried to use a comb to make his hair look less like Albert Einstein's. Neil was examining the equipment the girls had brought with them, and Justin was looking at the many scattered papers that were discarded on the floor with reckless abandon. Most of them were torn to shreds or simply aged to the point of being unreadable. One that he picked up seemed to contain a record of who was buried in which spot. The weird part was that there were two names under the same plot, and only one name had the initials O.G. next to it.

"That stands for the original grave. Creepy, huh?"

Sierra's voice came out of nowhere. She must have noticed Justin's interest in the scattered mess.

"Does this mean what I think it does?" Justin asked.

"Yup, bodies piled on top of bodies in almost all the plots out there. Some of the same ones were used maybe even four or five times, according to these records. That's why it's a good thing we're here. There are probably so many pissed-off spirits here that need closure."

"How, um, long have you been doing this, studying evil spirits?" Justin asked.

He was determined to keep the conversation going.

"Almost five years. I've had practice sessions with my elders before, but this is the first job I've done on my own. Usually, we film episodes on potion mixing and how properly ask to borrow materials from nature. I've never done a full cleansing before. That's why I was excited to find out about this place."

Justin looked at more of the records scattered about.

"Well, it looks like there's a lot of history to research here."

"That's exactly what we're about to get into with your friend over there."

Sierra said, flipping the hood on her cloak up and yelling "places!" to make sure everyone was ready to start filming.

"Ok," she told Angus, "We need you to come off like you're an expert on this place, even if you aren't yet."

He gave her an Okie Dokie sign with his fingers as Danielle continued to fight with his hairstyle.

"As for you two," She said, pointing fingers at Justin and Neil, "We will find a way to squeeze you into this. Maybe you're landscapers that have seen a whole bunch of crazy shit go down during your lunch break."

"You want us to make stuff up on the spot?" Justin asked.

"Just follow our lead," Danielle answered for her.

"Yeah, we don't want people knowing we did this illegally. We will feed you guys the lines. Then you can just stand back and watch us do our thing." Sierra said.

CHAPTER FIVE

They ventured back down to the basement, where so many bodies came in whole and left as a pile of dust. Danielle positioned Sierra and Angus, who were now wearing an ill-fitting sports jacket, in between the two furnaces. Justin almost thought about telling them that Between Two Furnaces should be the name of this episode of their web series. Katherine was explaining the cleansing ritual to Neil while landing him a small electronic device with a meter measured by a small needle. Justin listened to her explain how it worked to Neil while flipping through the old documents he had collected from the chapel earlier. One page caused Justin to freeze. It had the same markings as some of the tiny headstones they passed earlier. Graves that had been weathered by Mother Nature and were barely visible through the overgrown grass, but Justin remembered seeing the same drawing of a lamb and a teddy bear, only the ink on the paper had faded from time, distorting the figures and giving them faces that looked like they were screaming and in pain. For a brief second, Justin thought he heard the distant sound of a crying child. His skin turned cold, and he immediately tucked the record of child burials at the bottom of the stack.

The next one was a record of burials from as early as 1920. It was hard to believe it was that long ago. There was an article clipped to it from a newspaper about the opening of a special mausoleum built by a famous architect. The name was faded out, but the structure was beautiful. Its official name was The Wake House. It was probably the most redeeming part of the whole abandoned cemetery. Under that were more records, but nothing was too interesting until Justin came to a newspaper article from 1989 that read:

"Corpse abuse discovered in a local cemetery. Local gravedigger blows the whistle and reveals that up to 48,000 people were buried in graves already occupied."

Justin had a feeling Angus wasn't told about this when he shook the last caretaker's hand. This place had more history than he knew. He would have approached him about his findings, but Danielle had already called for everyone to be silent. Filming for their video had begun. It took a minute to figure out that the reason they were back down in the basement was to redo the intro to include Angus this time.

" Here we are at a very haunted location. This crematorium was the predecessor of a modern-day funeral home. Located on the back of a cemetery ripe with allegations of corpse abuse and frightening spectral encounters." Sierra began. She then motioned to Angus, who stood there still, looking confused at what he was supposed to say when it was his turn to talk.

"I'm standing here with the new caretaker who recently took on this place willingly, even after finding out about its dark history! This cemetery was mismanaged until its decline and abandonment in the 1980s. Isn't this true? "

"Um, yeah," Angus said.

"How incredibly brave. Even after all reports of reused graves, some of them so shallow that when it rained, the coffins would be left sticking out in plain sight. Some even said that wild hogs would even have to be chased off after breaking in and munching on the corpses. Then there were the matters of unidentifiable parts being found in garbage cans, cremated remains mixed together, and all the families that were victims of deception. I would say you have your hands full with some restless and angry specters."

"Sure do," Angus said. He was playing along, but his lines were coming out flat and unconvincing. They were going to have to do more takes. Justin could practically see Danielle cringe behind the camera.

"That's why I…called you guys in." He added, trying to improvise and save the scene.

"And you'll be glad you did!" Sierra said, walking over and putting her hand on Katherine's shoulder. "Because my partner and I are going to clear all of the negative energy out of here and restore this place to peace tonight! Starting with this room since it's the center of all the activity. Isn't that right, Kathrine?"

"That's right. I can feel the pain and sorrow moving through me as we speak." Katherine confirmed, motioning with her hands and feeling around for the strongest starting point. She naturally stopped at the furnaces and, as if completely in sync, Sierra followed her lead, and they both closed their eyes and put their hands on the graffiti-stained ovens. Slowly, quietly, they started to chant.

"Evil spirits, standing tall,

It's the time you've made your greatest fall,

We banish you with all our might,

Return to hell thou evil plight,

Go away and leave my sight,

And take with you this endless night."

They repeated this another time, they were going for a third, but right before they got to the banishing evil to hell part, Danielle cut them off by yelling, "Shit!" Louder than she probably meant to.

Sierra and Danielle snapped out of their trance, looking disappointed.

"Fuck Danielle, we almost had it. What happened?" Katherine

asked.

"My camera battery died, and I left the charger in the car."

The feeling of disappointment passed through the trio of the self-proclaimed "paranormal experts." Angus finally broke character and couldn't contain his laughter, causing Neil also to burst out. Justin started to feel uneasy. It was a good thing Danielle was going to retrieve her battery; he was in an even bigger hurry to get out of there now. He watched Danielle walk up the concrete ramp, and the little machine they had Neil holding suddenly jumped to life. The light lit up Neil's face, and the needle shot to the end of the meter.

"Uh oh." We got activity, he said, still joking.

Sierra and Katherine's eyes widened. "Danielle!" They called the only person that knew the equipment. She was almost out of the metal door before there was a loud thud, and Danielle screamed.

"The door just shut itself!" She yelled back. They could hear her repeatedly slam her hand against it in panic.

"You might wanna get back down here fast!" Sierra said.

Danielle came back and saw the meter going off the charts in Neil's hands and snatched it from him. Even Angus was at a loss for words and was looking around for someone to do something. Justin dropped the papers, and they all gathered closer to Danielle.

"Something's here, and it's pissed off." She informed them.

"Maybe you should do that chant again," Angus suggested

Sierra and Katherine looked at each other and considered this.

"It's gonna take a little more than that." They told him.

"We better find another way out of here and fast," Justin said, just as something in the furnace started banging against the closed door, trying to escape.

CHAPTER SIX

Whatever was in there was kicking frantically. With every bang, the mechanism shook violently. Thick clouds of dust, with bits of people still in it, blew in every direction. They all stayed together, stepping back but not looking away.

"What the fuck is happening here?" Angus asked. The noises came to a sudden stop, and the room fell silent.

"Well, it's clear that we might have woke something up with our little party." Neil chimed in.

Then the furnace groaned, echoing through the room. The room that had them trapped within. Everything in it was alive. Everything in it had a voice, and none of those voices had anything good to say. Justin started thinking about the window upstairs in the chapel. They could get out through that if they found a way to climb down. He didn't have a chance to speak up before Angus said, "screw this, there's no way something in there is alive." He was heading toward the furnace that, earlier, wouldn't come open.

"You three-set this up too, didn't you? Is this part of the video?" He asked the three paranormal experts. They all shook their heads no.

"Dude, I wouldn't do that if I were you," Justin told him. Of course, it was merely a suggestion, they all wanted to know what the banging was, but the rest of them were too scared to move.

So Angus slowly approached the rusty door and pulled up on the handle. This time it did lift, and sticking out were a pair of feet wearing shabby work boots. This person was probably a squatter, Justin thought. This guy picked the worst possible place to sleep and somehow managed to get himself stuck.

"What's going on?" The squatter asked in a scared, weak voice.

"Lance!?" Angus said, bending down to make sure he wasn't imagining things. "What the hell are you doing in there? Someone help me pull him out."

Justin and Angus each grabbed a leg and gently pulled Lance out of the mouth of the human-cooking oven. He was so heavily caked in ashes that it looked like he was wearing it as a costume. His bald head even had an ash toupee. It fell off of him and created clouds of death when he sat up.

"Lance, how did you get stuck in there?" Angus asked.

Lance looked around through squinted eyes. After adjusting to being back out in the light, he looked around the room at the faces he didn't recognize, back to Angus, whom he also no longer seemed to recognize.

"The last thing I remember is coming in here to get some things. Then I heard this sound. It sounded like someone crying, coming right out of this furnace. So I opened it up, and I swear to you, something pulled me in. It was like I was being held down by ten people at once. The voice stopped crying, and it whispered to me that it was… hungry."

Lance seemed like he wanted to say more but broke into a vicious cough. Angus patted him on the back.

"Does anyone have any water?" He asked before realizing the others, aside from Justin, were all trying to open the big door that was jammed. Justin realized that he meant to grab water and sports drinks earlier, but in his pocket was a tall can of lukewarm beer. He purchased it without a second thought. He supposed he thought he was gonna need to at least stay buzzed through this whole experience. Never mind that now.

"Um, I have this," he said, handing the brew to Lance.

The old man popped it open and gulped it down as if he had just trekked through the desert for days without a drop to drink. It seemed to bring a little life back into him. He chucked the can against the wall and hopped to his feet.

"So, what's going on here? Who are all these people?" He asked Angus.

"Well, I originally was just gonna bring my friend Justin here to show him around, and we invited our new friend Neil over there for our muscle, but then we found those lovely ladies trying to help get the main door open over there, but it slammed shut and locked or something. Don't worry, though. They're paranormal experts, and they are trying to cleanse this place of negative energy or something like that." Angus answered.

Lance squinted his eyes, and for a second, Justin could swear that something in them changed for a split second. It was like a second set of eyes dropped down over his normal ones, and those eyes were cloudy and lifeless. They were gone again in an instant. Angus was wondering why the others couldn't get the door open yet. He yelled for them to just come back down, telling them that Lance would probably know how to do it. He had his back turned to Justin and Lance, and only Justin could see that Lance was now licking the ashes of the dead off of his arm. Clumps of it caked his tongue, and he rolled it back into his mouth and swallowed all of it. Justin stood there in shock and couldn't think of what to say. Deep in his mind, he knew he should say something; this was getting too weird, too fast. He couldn't make up his mind on what was real and what wasn't. The past two days had been full of alcohol-fueled visions. He worried that he finally drank himself crazy.

"Such an interesting combination of flavors," Lance said to Him.

He wiped his mouth like someone who just finished eating a gourmet meal.

"Just think of all those people bound together in the dust, someone's grandmother, someone's son or daughter, parents, teachers, politicians. All dirt now."

Lance's eyes changed again, the kindness was gone entirely, and something in his face jerked and contorted his features into something otherworldly. A sound like twigs being snapped in half came from his mouth, his cheeks sunk in, and his teeth separated themselves from his jaw and pushed forward. Veins popped out of his head like thick lighting bolts.

Justin backed up as the ghoulish figure advanced toward him.

"Hey, you guys!" He called to the crew, but they couldn't hear him.

"You won't leave here alive," possessed Lance told him. "Your bodies will burn, but your soul will remain here as just another shadow crawling along the walls."

"Hey, someone come help me; I think Lance has lost his mind!" Justin shouted again.

Danielle and Katherine were trying to get a signal on their cell phone. They weren't paying attention. Angus, Neil, and Sierra came to see why Justin was yelling. Judging from the look on their faces, Justin could tell he wasn't the only one seeing the demon-eyed caretaker, who had walked back to the furnace and whispered to it in an unrecognizable language. Then his head snapped back towards the others. " It's time for the mouth of hell to open again," Lance said aloud to everyone in the room. Danielle and Katherine had joined them after unsuccessfully trying to call anyone on their phones.

"Well, we are not getting out of here anytime soon," Katherine said; she noticed that they didn't hear a word she said, then followed their attention to the old man.

"That's right, there is no way out, not until its hunger has been suppressed," Lance said, petting the furnace

"Now, who wants to go first and see what awaits you on the other side?"
He gestured to the open furnace, and somewhere in the back of the infinite darkness, a bright red ball of light formed. It was the beginning of a fire.

CHAPTER SEVEN

Did they all just hear him refer to the furnace as if it were a living thing? Like it was some sort of powerful entity? He even asked the thing if it was hungry in the same soft-spoken tone a parent would use with a child. "I finally found you some more food," he told it. Everyone stood in place, dumb stricken, until Lance turned to them and stared at them with the eyes of a predatory animal. That was enough to let them know that they were what he referred to as "the food."

He quickly lunged at them before they could make the first move and caught Katherine by the arm first. They all grabbed him at once and tried to pull her out of his grasp, but the old man proved to be stronger than they anticipated. Katherine delivered a hard kick to his gut. When the long heel of her shoe connected with his stomach, it went straight through the skin and punctured a hole. She pulled it back out, and his intestines came spilling out, tangling her leg in a mess of slimy, muscular tubes. Neil came from behind and delivered a swift, hard punch to the side of his head, caving it in. That was still not enough to stop the monster. Demon Lance projectile vomited grey ash straight onto Katherine's face, covering her mouth and eyes in it.

She gasped for breath while Danielle and Sierra pulled her foot out of the maze of guts. Neil, Angus, and Justin worked together to restrain the man-thing that should not have still been alive.

"It's so hungry," Lance growled, his teeth falling out one by one and sliding down his chin. " We won't let you leave until it's satisfied again."

"Did he just say we?" Neil asked.

"Keep holding him. We need to find something to tie him down with." Angus said.

Justin studied the old man with horror. He was moving, but somehow he looked like he was dead before they found him. He even noticed that there were deep gashes straight down his wrist like he had cut himself with a razor blade. Lance had a deep red mark that went all the way around his neck; he had tried several times to kill himself and couldn't make it work, Justin thought.

As if he had read Justin's mind, Lance slowly turned his head toward him and smiled.

"We couldn't let him die until the right time. We needed him to lure you here. Oh, this host tried his best to stop the progress, but we eventually got through to him." As Lance said this, his voice changed tones. First dropping real low, then becoming shrill and hoarse. Then it started cracking, transforming into maniacal laughter. The temperature around them rose quickly to unbearable degrees. That's when they noticed the old man was suddenly becoming lighter. He was shrinking; all of his insides were now spilling out of the hole in his stomach like they were being sucked out. His liver, lungs, bladder, intestines, liver, and kidneys were all on the floor in a messy pile. This continued until his eyeballs and brain followed, creating a topper on the world's most disgusting cake. Neil, Angus, and Justin were now only holding a loose rubbery pile of hollowed-out human skin and bones. Neil gagged and threw it. There was a loud slapping sound when it hit the wall on the other side of them. It stuck to the concrete for a second, then slowly, inch by inch, it slid down until it was in a sitting position, like a child's toy, in the corner of the room. The flesh doll jerked its head back up despite having no bone structure for support, its hollow eyes narrowed, and it laughed at them again.

"Do you feel it burning through you yet? It's going to melt you down and digest you whole." Beads of sweat were starting to pour from their faces. They realized where the heat was coming from. It was the furnace, and not only was it putting out extreme heat, but it also made a low growling sound. Justin pictured it sprouting to life, growing legs, and charging at them. He meant to warn them that they needed to run back upstairs, but being in shock would only allow him to say it in a barely audible voice. They did move, but it all seemed like the whole sequence seemed to move at dream speed. All of time and space were slowed down, but they all managed to make it back to the stairway. It was the only route away from the room full of nightmares below them.

"Wait, isn't heat supposed to rise?" Angus pointed out.

He was right. That was usually the case. However, as they climbed the stairs, the air turned cold and stale. They had ascended from the pits of hell and reached the chapel room again. Sierra ushered them inside but remained on guard at the entranceway.

"Katherine, toss me the salt!" She called. A plastic jar, filled with thick salt, and covered with strange markings hand-drawn on the outside, landed right in the palm of Sierra's hand. She started around the entrance to the room and went all the way around, creating a white line barrier the length of the circular room.

"Does she think that will keep us safe?"Angus asked. "We're like sitting ducks in here."

"Right now, I don't think it could hurt to try," Katherine replied. Her wide eyes stuck out like two gems against the grey and black mess that covered her face.

Danielle was once again trying to find a cellphone connection. Justin looked for windows. Maybe if he could get one open, They could rig something up to climb down. The problem was that there was only one. It was a stained glass window, which he considered smashing open with something. He was going to see if Angus and Neil could find a solid enough object to break through it, but an excited shout from Danielle drew all their attention to her.

"I got through. I got 911 on the phone!"

She started laying out the situation and location to the dispatcher, leaving out the more weird parts about how the man sitting just below them died. Justin thought that was wise. Any of those details would have caused them to automatically write it off as a prank phone call and hang upon them. Plus, they still hadn't got the chance to talk about what they had just experienced with a clear head and whether or not it was hysteria. Whatever it was, it made Justin feel like he was, once again, trapped in a hungover fever dream.

Danielle hung up the phone. Sierra completed her salt circle and was chanting something with her eyes closed.

"How long did they say it would take them to get here?" Katherine asked

Danielle looked displeased with the answer that she was about to have to give.

"Forty-five minutes to an hour." She told them.

They all shared a look of helplessness.

"Fuck" Angus said. "I guess we better buckle down for a bit."

"Now I wish I had my guitar. Working on music might take my mind on what's left of that shriveled-up dead guy down there," Neil added.

"Yeah, we not gonna discuss that any further?" Justin asked.

"All I can say for sure is that this is on a whole other level than anything we've dealt with before. I wish we made contact, but that might be too dangerous." Sierra answered. "We should just stay inside of our safety circle and not do anything to draw any more attention to our presence until someone comes for us."

CHAPTER EIGHT

Waiting for their rescue in silence made the minutes turn into excruciatingly long hours. Only a little over sixty minutes had passed with no signs of hope. Justin knew from the distant look in Angus' eyes and the way he was chewing on his bottom lip that he was holding back on his emotions. Angus was never one to share his feelings unless it was joyful. He told Justin once that he grew up being told to walk tall under any circumstances. Show no weakness.

"I'm sorry your cemetery caretaker and haunted attraction thing didn't work out, man," Justin said.

He squatted down against the wall next to his friend, trying to be comforting. Angus kept looking into the space as if he was watching his hopes and ambitions being projected right in front of him like a movie, things that could have been.

"I thought I was going to be able to save the last interesting thing from the history of this town," Angus replied. "Now, because of me, we're all stuck here, and you know what? I don't think anyone is coming to get us. I'm not even sure that girl talked to emergency services. Think about it; it doesn't make sense that she's the only one left with her phone intact."

He was right. To keep themselves from going crazy thinking about the sack of skin that used to be a man currently rotting in the basement, they naturally turned to their phones to pass the time faster, only to discover melted chunks of plastic in their pockets. Somehow this had happened during their flee to safety.

"Maybe it's because she got up here before us," Justin offered.

"I think it's false hope. that was this place playing a trick on us."Angus replied, then added, "We are going to die here."

Those words hit Justin like a punch to the gut. In this short amount of time, his friend had utterly lost every ounce of optimism that he was known for. He didn't know the others since he had just met them, but they all seemed like they were also growing more distressed by the minute. Justin thought that maybe it was because he had spent the past few days hibernating in his hell that he was the only one able to think rationally after what they just went through. Did they just all witness a guy's insides dissolve? Or was it only Justin who saw that because that's what his mind made him see?

"We are getting out of here," Justin assured him.

He looked to the other four. He had to bring up what he was sure they were all thinking.

"Was I the only one who saw that guy's insides melt out of his skin?" He asked them.

"It all happened so fast, but one thing for sure," Danielle said, pointing at Katherine. "Her foot went right through him."

Katherine held out her shoe; it was still covered in something sticky, alright.

"Somehow, our chanting pissed off whatever is in here," Sierra chimed in. "It woke up every vile malevolent spirit in this place, and now they won't let us leave until we give them something."

"Bullshit," Angus argued. "You all felt how hot it got down there. Some kind of pipe must have burst, and the door swelled shut. It happens all the time. Then we must have breathed in some sort of gas, and it's making us slowly go crazy."

"You don't know shit," Sierra shot back at him.

"Yeah, you haven't seen some of the things we have, things that can't be explained with logic, only they've never gotten this bad," Katherine added.

Angus scoffed, causing the girls to raise their voices over his, and Justin was about to tell them all to calm down before Neil cut them all off.

"Guys, shut up. I found something over here!"

Justin went to where Neil was squatting in front of a crescent-shaped hole. The jagged symmetry made it look like it was carved with a dull knife. The top of something was sticking out of it. There were three small buttons on top of the object. One was marked with a red dot, one with a sideways triangle, and the last one with a square. The words below them were too faded out to read.

"I know the record, play, and stop buttons when I see them," Neil said. "It's some sort of recording device. I need something to pry it out with."

"I have nails; let me give it a try," Katherine said.

She stuck her long, plastic fake nails down in the hole, using them like tweezers. The blood-red nail polish scrapped off by the inch as she fought to wiggle the device loose. It took a few minutes, but she managed to do it without breaking a single one-off. The tape recorder was unstuck, but before getting it out, Katherine yelped in pain, quickly jerking her hand back. The tip of her index finger had a thick, sharp splinter coming out of it.

"Fuck!" She cried. Neil finished pulling the tape recorder out while Sierra helped try to look for something to treat Katherine's finger. There was still a small cassette tape in it. Although Neil doubted they would be able to listen to it.

"This thing is ancient by today's standards." He noted. "The batteries in it are probably warped as shit. There's no way this thing will play."

"Try it anyway." Justin urged.

He was anxious to hear what was on it.

"Yeah," Angus agreed solemnly." Let's see if we can hear the sounds of death and agony on there."

"Maybe there's something useful about another way out of here on it." Danielle chimed in. Justin was glad she had some hope. Cause the rest of theirs were fading fast.

Neil pressed the play button. There was a clicking sound, and that was it.

"That's what I thought." He said.

They were all disappointed that the evening's entertainment that would help the passing time was a bust. Neil tossed the tape recorder, and it landed with a thud on the floor, and something inside of it kicked into motion. The sounds of garbled, distorted nonsense in slow motion filled the room but slowly adjusted into the sound of a man speaking in secret, with his voice barely above a whisper. Justin couldn't process how the voice could sound both in the distant past and with them in the present at the same time. It was like he was right there with them as a ghost. One that was there to relay a message.

CHAPTER NINE

Whispering voice (sounding very frightened): *Hello, I hope this thing is recording because this is the last thing I'll ever record. What's about to take place here tonight very well could be the beginning of the end—the end of everything.*

(Strange rhythmic chanting begins in the background)

Voice: *ok, my name is Burden Jinx, or at least that's the name they gave me. For the past few months, I've taken refuge in this abandoned crematorium that sits on a cemetery. The people I've been staying with, I think they are some sort of cult. At first, I joined them because I was tired of sleeping on the streets. I didn't know who they were. I was told that all I had to do was be in charge of recording their lessons. They seemed so harmless. Then they started talking about demons and raising one in the old furnace in the basement. They said it was perfect since this place has such a dark history filled with debauchery.*

Then there were other acts that I wished I had never witnessed. Every week they performed a ritual that they called The Blood Circus. They covered themselves in blood. Probably from animals that were found roaming the area, those poor souls. After coloring themselves crimson red, they would take turns performing lewd acts in front of the furnace. Some would just pleasure themselves, then please a partner. Often this would turn into a full-blown orgy. Some would shit on the floor and then rub ejaculate on their hands and face, mixing it in with the blood, all of which I was forced to record on this damn tape recorder. Afterward, they would throw the tape in the furnace like a sacrifice. I'm not sure what this was supposed to accomplish, but I would be surprised if this caused the place to be, well, cursed.

(Chanting slowly dies out in the background)

Burden Jinx: *Oh no, they've gone quiet. That's not good. I'm hiding in the chapel because they never come up here. They said that they like it better down there until they've desecrated everything holy in this place. That's why they said that they will sacrifice themselves to it, and by IT, I mean that they think that there is the spirit of a demon god in the furnace that was used to burn bodies in. I watched them, night after night, offering things to it. They brought it dead squirrels and birds that they found around the cemetery, but they said it wasn't enough. It wasn't satisfied; it wasn't good enough for it to give them the gift of fire straight from hell. I should explain. Supposedly when the furnace burns with fire, that means the demon was satisfied. Then, after they throw themselves into it and let it swallow them, they come back immortal. It's crazy, and I don't want to be here anymore, but now they won't let me leave.*

(The distant sound of a small bell ringing)

Distant voice: *The time has come. The flames will rise! Everyone gathers around. The beast has spoken. It says our time has come. We will not die in vain!*

Burden Jinx: *Shit! They're going to come looking for me. I don't want to be a part of this. They think they can summon creatures from the underworld that they'll die and come back. I'm not hearing it; there's nothing after death. I wish they had never talked to me. If someone hears this tape, you'll know what happened. I was murdered by a group of madmen.*

(The ringing of the bell grows louder)

Burden Jinx: *Ok, I'm gonna go quiet until they pass.*

(Static feedback and the sounds of light, rhythmic breathing)

Female voice (Sweet and singsong): *Oh Jinx, where are you? We have something so spectacular to show you. You have to come to take a record of this! The time has come for the bright flame to burn. Into the fire we go!*

(Breathing on the recording intensifies as the sound of footsteps grows closer)

Female voice*: Oh, come on, Burden. Why are you hiding? Is it because you know that you're the weakest link in our chain? That you might not be granted the chance to come back from the darkness? You know that's how we chose your moniker, right? You've done nothing to show your allegiance here; you've only been in our way. Now is the chance to prove yourself. Come out now, coward!*

(The sounds of shuffling and breathing getting heavier. Something falls and makes a loud crashing sound.)

Burden Jinx(whispering): *Shit!*

Female voice: *Ha! There he is. Damn you for making us come into this forsaken place! Grab him by his other leg, Caleb. We can't do this without the right number of sacrifices.*

Burden Jinx: *Please, no! I don't want to be a part of this. It's gone too far! We are all going to die here! Death is the end. There's no coming back! If you think there is, you're crazy. You're all crazy!*

Male voice(Caleb?): *I can't get his other leg. The little fucker is too slippery!*

Female voice: *You're a big boy. Knock him out if you have to. We don't have much time.*

(Burden Jinx screams as the sickening thud of fist against flesh echos off the mic. This continues until the screaming comes to a sudden stop.)

Male voice: *Alright, He's out.*

Female voice: *Good, I didn't want to spend the time up here dragging him kicking and screaming. We need to save our energy for more important things.*

(The voices get fainter, and the sounds of Burden's unconscious body being drug across the floor can be heard.)

Male voice: *You promise that this will satisfy the great ones?*

Female voice: *In all of my time leading this group, have I been wrong yet?*

Male voice: *You've got me there.*

(The voices go completely out of range for a full three minutes. The only thing heard is Burden's head hitting each stair on the way down)

Female voice (faint but distressed): *Wait, what's this? You idiots! You weren't supposed to go before me. Do you realize what you've done? The ritual is ruined! Our souls will be trapped here forever! Spare us, dark Lords! Let's try the process again! The next time we will do better. We will find more sacrifices, better ones!*

(A loud rumble drowns out the audio of what happens next, but as the tape comes to an end, the female voice can be heard screaming, followed by static, and the tape clicks as it comes to an end.)

CHAPTER TEN

Angus paced briskly across the floor behind the group, who were discussing what they had just heard.

"So they murdered him, right? We just heard a tape of a cult killing someone and probably committing mass suicide." Angus said.

"In a cemetery where dead people were piled in mass graves on top of each other," Justin added.

Everyone's eyes turned to him.

"What?" Sierra asked

"Oh yeah, on top of this place being a clubhouse for demon worshipping, it turns out that the people running this cemetery have also been shady as fuck from the beginning," Justin said, gesturing to the files scattered about. "It's all on record."

Sierra and Katherine started picking up the papers and looking over them.

"Holy shit. You're right. That's why this place is such a vortex of negative energy. It's the perfect place to conjure a demon." Katherine confirmed.

"Ok, but we need to focus on how we get out of here then," Neil added.

"There's no way we are getting that door open down there," Danielle said to him. "You might as well wait for someone to come."

"It's been over an hour, though. Do you think they're still coming? Get real." He argued with her. "Screw this staying in the circle stuff. There has to be another way out, and I'm gonna find it."

"I was thinking about breaking open that stained glass window, and we could find some way to repel it down," Justin told him.

"Sounds good to me."

"I don't think any of you understand. This thing, and these dwelling spirits that were left here. They are powerful, and we won't get out here until it finishes its business. We just have to find out what it wants us to do." Sierra said.

"Like a seance?" Katherine asked, " I don't know if I'm ready for that yet."

Sierra took both of Katherine's hands in hers. She looked at her, reassuring her with her eyes.

"You can do this, I promise. I'm good at cleansing and your good at communicating, remember?"

"But this place is so dark, so angry."

The confidence Katherine had displayed earlier that night was gone now.

"Look, remember when we cleansed the evil energy out of that abandoned house where they arrested that group of people that thought they were real vampires?" Sierra asked. "That was some heavy stuff. They found the bodies of people who were murdered and drained of their blood in that place. If you can make it through that, I know you can make it through this too."

Katherine's face turned paler than it already was. Justin wondered what memories could be taken from exploring a real-life murder house.

"There were still marks on the linoleum floor in the kitchen made by one of their victim's fingernails. You could still make out the horrible things they wrote in their victim's blood on the wall. We tried to speak to the victims through me, but the voice speaking through me turned out to be one of the vampire people. I could see him in my mind while he used me. He died trying to attack the cops. I remember seeing the bullet hole dripping with dark red goop. I still feel him in there sometimes. I'll suddenly get a headache and run to the mirror, expecting to see my skull cracking open. With his eye peeking out of it. I can't go through that again."She said.

"I promise it will be different this time. You just didn't have the experience points back then." Sierra assured her.

Katherine took in her words, thought about it, then reluctantly agreed.

"We better get this on record, though. Danielle, did you bring the backup camera?"

"You mean the action camera? Yeah, it has night vision too."

"Great, we'll use that," Sierra said. "Everyone else, you're gonna act as our witnesses, and you might need to help restrain her."

Katherine said nothing, but her facial expression did not hide her regret.

"So, you're just gonna bargain with this thing? Ask it to let us go if you do it a favor?" Angus asked.

"Something like that, although it's more like we figure out its weakness so we can expel it," Sierra told him. "As long as we stay in this circle, we have it in a controlled environment where it doesn't have power, but it will try to use Katherine as a vessel to deal physical damage. That's why you guys must hold her down."

Katherine went directly to the center of the room and laid down flat on the floor while Sierra did some kind of high-pitched chant. Danielle fished out her small action camera and attached it to a little handheld tripod. Neil positioned himself at Katherine's head, Angus at her right arm, Justin at her feet. Danielle took the left arm after she was done setting up the video equipment. Sierra rubbed a clear oil on a larger candle and lit the wick. She began to dance around them, continuously picking up speed until the candlelight became a yellow blur. The quicker Sierra moved, the more the yellow flame revealed the faces that were graffitied on the wall, and it gave off the illusion that they were moving. Like images in a flipbook, the faces that were painted white lost their color until their flesh turned the same black as rotten fruit. Justin could picture a hole opening in that rot and little beads of white appearing as maggots burst through and rained down onto them.

He shivered at the thought, then Katherine started convulsing. Her eyes rolled into the back of her head until all that could be seen were two white marbles. A gurgling sound rose from her throat.

"Is she choking?" Angus asked, sounding panicked.

"Don't break away!" Sierra commanded.

Although it wasn't them that broke the ritual, it was the sound of the bay door below them opening and the sound of a comforting voice calling "hello." Justin was glad to see Katherine's eyes return. She shot up to her feet, and they did too.

"Holy shit, we're saved!" Danielle shouted. "I gotta pack our equipment back up. Don't leave without me!"

They promised not to. They excitedly exited the chapel, Justin asked Danielle if she needed help, but she insisted that she didn't. Before leaving the salt circle, he did step over it extra cautiously, just in case. He did want any sort of lingering presence to get ahold of her before they were free. He couldn't wait for them to make it out of here alive and have a weird story to tell someday.

CHAPTER ELEVEN

The basement of death was still as hot as the inside of an oven and still reeked of rotten meat. They ran as fast as they could towards the voice. The person had to be coming down the ramp now to greet them. They would be found soon enough, but Angus still yelled, "Right here, don't let that door shut!" The worst-case scenario was for their rescue to get stuck too.

The night air could be felt against their faces, and the feeling of freedom and the relief of this night being over. Justin thought about how they could just go drink back in the van and forget it ever happened. They would become rational again and come up with a sane explanation for what they saw earlier that was not a man whose insides were not spilled out of a foot-sized orifice in his body. That would all be behind them.

"Hello, is anyone in here?" Asked the faceless voice once again.

"Yes!" They all yelled at the same time.

"Can they not hear us? Why haven't they come in here yet? Did you tell them there's a dead body down there?" Angus asked Danielle.

They reached the ramp, and each of their hopes died in an instant. The door was still shut. Maybe the fire department couldn't get the door open from the outside, Justin thought. Maybe they were calling from the other side. Maybe they needed to be louder to be heard. Then, the same voice called, this time it was from inside the room somewhere. It felt like it was right behind them.

"What the hell?" Said Neil. "Dude, if you let that door close behind you, then You're screwed too."

"It's no worries, just follow my voice. I'll have us out of here in a split second." The voice said.

Whoever they were sounded like they knew what they were doing, so they did as they were told and followed the voice back down the ramp. The basement was still empty; even the pile of flesh wasn't in the corner anymore. Did someone already move it?

"Yeah, if you guys already found the, um, what was left of that guy, you could understand how badly we want out of here. So maybe just tell us where you're at?" Angus said.

There was a silence until something gelatinous shuffled across the floor and trotted past them in the blink of an eye, then the lights flickered out.

"It was a fucking trick. We should have known better! Go, go, go!" Sierra commanded.

They couldn't tell which way to go in the pitch black. The heat was now so intense that Justin felt that he would melt right into the floor and be stuck in here for the rest of eternity. He wondered if the others were feeling it too. He was sure of it when the sudden eerie glow from a yellow flame lit up the room. He could see their sweating faces. It was the furnace coming to life, the fire was burning again, and it had them right where it wanted them. They were arranged in an almost perfect circle around it without them even being aware of the formation. They all slowly started to back away from the incinerator. Pain from a sudden leg cramp stopped Justin on the spot, and he fell backward.

"The sweat in my eyes, I can't see anything." Katherine cried out.

Danielle was frozen in place; she went to speak, but only an exasperated gasp escaped her mouth, and she felt her cheeks appear to sink into her face like sand. Her whole body was drying out and weakening. Sierra was digging through her bag before whatever was affecting everyone else reached her. She took out a small notebook when the whole thing turned as red as a lump of heated coal and burned her. She dropped it and watched as tiny blisters formed all over her palms. She bit down on her lip to keep the scream in. She wouldn't let the evil have the satisfaction of hearing the sounds of her agony.

Angus was stumbling around like a sleepwalker.

"If you guys don't mind, I'm just gonna crash here." He said before collapsing on the ground and going out cold.

"Angus!" Justin called, trying to will him back into consciousness. He was practically stuck in place, lying on his back. There was a sound approaching him that he couldn't see. It was like the hooves of a giant animal stomping across wet pavement. And a shadow appeared in the corner of his eye, not revealing itself until it was almost right over his head. A massive wild hog was stalking them with a piece of Lance's face hanging off of one of its tusks. Something else hung out of the side of its mouth; as it got closer, it appeared to be half of a hand. Each finger was chewed down to the bone, and they were wiggling around like they were still attached to a living being. The pig's face was strange-looking. Half of it was bloated, and a half was decayed; its skull could be seen from the top of its head down to its unhinged jaw. Two glowing red eyes looked straight up, and its gaping mouth was wide open and like a large black hole ready to suck the world and everything in it into oblivion. There was a momentary glimpse of something trying to make its way out of that hole, and for just enough time to scream "help me," Neil did manage to stick his entire face out.

Oh no, it swallowed Neil like a God damn snake would swallow its food whole, Justin thought. All of us are incapacitated to a certain degree that we've all been rendered useless. The close the thing moved to the fire, the more obvious the reason was that it had to take the fight out of them. It was going to have its first meal in a long time. Neil was fighting. The shape of his hands and feet could be made out trying to puncture through its belly. Then, using itself as a vessel, it hoisted itself into the furnace with Neil still inside. His screams echoed off the walls as he burned alive, then faded out with his existence. After it was over, the voice spoke again, at first sounding like the person they heard earlier that they hoped was there to rescue them, then slowing down like the warped recording on the tape. They realized now that's where the voice was coming from. It was the furnace, of whatever inhabited the furnace, speaking to them.

"Those of you who opened the door, don't be afraid to follow behind your friend. Submit your soul to me, and I will have mercy on you, and your death with be swift and less painful." It said.

CHAPTER TWELVE

The flame grew both brighter and hotter. Justin felt the feeling come back to his feet, and he was able to stand again. He ran over to a barely conscious Angus and put a hand under each of his arms. His friend was not light, so he drugs him across the floor, not knowing how he would get him back to the only logical place to go, back up the stairs.

"We have to get back into the circle!" Sierra said as if she was reading his mind.

He was way ahead of her. He noticed that she was guiding Katherine with both hands wrapped up in torn-off pieces of her shirt. The young medium was still trying to clear her vision. Her eyes were swollen, causing her to squint permanently. Danielle was gasping for breath; her skin was dry and sunk in around her cheekbones. She followed behind them, moving weakly. Justin thankfully got Angus conscious enough to walk on his own as they climbed back up into the chapel. Right before they crossed over the barrier, Justin felt like he was going to collapse again. However, he refused and forced himself to pick up a folding chair that was propped up against the wall. He went over to where the giant face was painted around the stained glass and watched him with solemn eyes.

He was pretty sure that it wasn't there earlier. Now a giant oblong face, painted with dark green, leaving only blank spots for eyes, circled the window. It left the stained glass pattern looking like colorful jagged teeth in an open mouth.

"Sorry," he said before smashing through the lower half of the figure's mouth. Where he was met with the sight of the second layer of stained glass with almost the same design, only more grotesque teeth were more open in this version, circling the dark pit of an open mouth. Inside that mouth was a smaller, darker hole that looked like an open wound. Justin leaned in closer to examine it to see if he could see what was beyond. With one eye squinted, he looked into the small bottomless circle, and something small wiggled its way out of it. It was like a living piece of white thread dancing its way out, followed by another and another until there were a dozen of them Wiggling their way right into Justin's iris. They moved so fast that he could practically feel them work their way in between his eyelids before he swatted at them, and his hand found nothing.

The mouth hole began puckering and making a wolf-whistling sound before a tiny, shrill voice said Justin's name.

"Hey Justin, you know what to do when you see a hole in a wall, don't ya? You look like you could use a little action. I'll tell you what, if you agree to go down there and give yourself to the fire, I'll give you a parting gift you wouldn't believe. I'll suck you off something fierce. Come on, big boy, you know you want it."

This was followed by long, wet slurping and sucking sounds that turned Justin's stomach.

He jumped when Sierra popped up behind him to give him his candle.

"You're going to need this; if we wanna live, then we'll be here a while." She said.

"And can I ask what exactly we are gonna do now? That thing has us, prisoner, in here, and it's starting to use tactics for luring us back down there." Angus asked.

"We need to figure out its weakness and drain its energy. It's growing more powerful. The more it gets people to sacrifice themselves to it, the stronger it gets. I think that forcing it to speak through Katherine would be a horrible idea right now. We stand a better chance if we all work together and find a way so that each one of us can peak into the spiritual world at once and try to figure this thing out before it gets the rest of us." Sierra said

"So, you're thinking what I'm thinking?" Katherine asked

"Yup," Sierra said, " have you guys ever heard of astral projection?" She asked Justin and Angus hypothetically.

"Don't think I have," Justin told her.

"Astral projection? You mean pushing our spirit out of our buttholes?" Angus asked sarcastically.

Justin knew that Sierra would roll her eyes and throw her hands up at their level of immaturity.

"It's something like that," Danielle said quietly from the other side of the room.

"It's communicating with an entity that doesn't have a physical body to lead you through a vision of their realm."

"Yes!" Sierra said to her with a thumbs up. "It's like being conscious in your dreams. What we are going to do is put ourselves in a trance and ask to enter the spirit realm, which means we have to push our souls out of our bodies and use them to see things we'd otherwise be blind to, but you have to be open-minded and concentrate. Katherine can use her power to ask the spirits to let us all in."

"I'd say after everything that's happened tonight, every one of us will do anything to figure out a way out of here," Angus said.

"Good, so I'm going to draw something on the ground, and we all need to sit around it in a circle," Sierra said

The strange symbols she drew in chalk, something resembling a cross between Roman numerals and the English alphabet, were arranged in the same style that the letters appear on an Ouija board. They formed a tight circle around it and sat down crossed-legged with all hands joined.

"I want you to follow the sound of my voice," Katherine said loudly.

"The more I speak, the further away my voice will travel. I want you to close your eyes and feel yourself being pulled through the darkness and out to the other side with me."

They closed their eyes and let complete darkness wash over like a huge wave and lay itself on like a thick blanket. Justin felt like he was being sucked into a black hole. The force of its power yanked his soul out through the top of his head, and the only thing he could see was his physical body getting further and further away. The sound of Katherine's voice was faint at first and booming in the next second.

"Now, when I count down to one, everyone opens your eyes at once." She said. "Five, four, three, two…"

Then she was gone. Justin felt weightless and oddly relaxed. It was like he was untethered from all the problems he faced in the real world. He was free.

"One!" Katherine's voice called. Then he was slingshotted through another darkness where everything moved faster within a shorter period. He caught up with the rest of them within seconds. Standing above their physical selves.

CHAPTER THIRTEEN

Their outer selves sat as still as statues. Angus bent down to test whether or not his spiritual manifestation would go through his physical one. It did just that. When he stuck two spectral fingers through the back of his head, they came out of his eyes.

"Cool," he said, his voice not rising above a whisper.

"What now?" Justin asked.

His voice came out in the same whisper as Angus. This must have been the only volume you could speak in the dead world. Katherine pointed to the open door of the chapel. It was so full of red light that it looked like they were walking right into the core of a volcano.

"We can go anywhere we want; they can't see us unless we willingly choose to reveal ourselves," She told them.

Sierra stood frozen in place, glaring into the red inferno.

"Are you sure?" She asked. "We've never done this before. Are you sure they won't see us?"

"It's either find a solution this way, or we can wait here and die," Katherine said.

Sierra nodded in agreement and started to the stairs to lead the way with Katherine and Danielle. Angus and Justin slowly followed close behind, both exchanging "Can you believe this shit?" glances at each other.

Walking this way felt like walking on air. Justin noted that it felt like he was gliding down the stairs more than he was walking. He rubbed his hands along both sides of the wall. They felt fleshy and moist. Shadows danced along the wall and disappeared too quickly to be able to make out their form, but it felt way more claustrophobic than it did when they first arrived. The walls seemed closer together, and the path downward grew more narrow. The basement was a completely different scene. Gathered around the oven were very tall people. They had to be standing at least eight feet. They were dressed like undertakers, in suits, all black aside from red ties. Their faces were covered with black and grey dust. Human ashes are worn like a mask. They were holding lit torches in their glove-covered hands.

The incinerator was less like a machine and more like a sentient being trying to break free of its barriers. Each movement it made was met with a creaking sound. Each creaking sound was met with frustration and a growl coming from the possessed contraption. Two more suited people entered the room, escorting a person in a dirty brown robe. The hood was pulled up to hide their face. One of the suited-up people, whose amber-colored eyes were the only visible part of his face, ordered the newcomer to remove the robe. The figure brought their hands to the front of the robe and pulled it off in one swift motion. Before them stood a very burned and distorted version of what used to be Neil.

Thin strands of hair ran down one side of his charred, crooked, and now unrecognizable head. The only thing that was left from his previous self was the top half of his shirt that was melted to his torso as a permanent part of his body. His band's logo was still visible. All the rest was just one red, swollen mass. The undertaker with symbols etched on his face mask, who presumably was the leader, circled and examined Neil. He took his hands, extending his long boney fingers, and jabbed them into Neil's cheeks. The skin pulled back over his jawbone, creating a giant cartoonish smile. He then pulled his hands back to himself. The ends of his fingers were now covered in dark clumps. He smeared some on his face and put some on his tongue. He moved it around in his mouth, tasting it like a wine sample.

His lips twisted, his nostrils flared, and his facial expression turned sour. He spits an oily wad onto the floor. The substance sprang to life and started flopping like a dying fish until the lead undertaker stomped it out of existence. That was all the assurance the rest of the cult needed. They were testing to see whether Neil had what it took to join them, and he was rejected. They started tearing Neil apart piece by piece. Parts of his body were tossed to the side until he was reduced to just a head and torso. Two of the cult members were each holding one of his arms and legs with sharp pieces of broken bone sticking out. They jammed the ligaments into the wrong places on his body. The new version of the former metalhead was now two feet tall, and the cult members pushed him and kicked him like a group of schoolyard bullies.

Then without hesitation, ash face picked up bite-sized Neil, whispered something into his ear, and threw him back into the incinerator. Justin didn't know if the others could hear it as well as he did, but he heard shrieking coming inside the fire.

"What happens when they put them back in?" He asked Sierra.

She shrugged.

Their answer came when a geyser of red and black chunks shot back out of the fire woodchipper style. Even the fire demon rejected the sacrifice. The rest of the suited cult members cleaned the mess. So it was clear they were slaves in the afterlife. Their main purpose was to serve the fire.

"What do we do now?" Angus asked.

"Nothing," Katherine told him. "If we break away from each other or draw attention to ourselves, they could see us and know we can see them. We just wanna observe and see if they give us anything to work with."

"Hold on, look at this," Sierra told them.

She was referring to the leader. He had picked up a thick strip of Neil's flesh off the floor that was still soaking with blood. He went to the furnace and lifted the part of the machine where the metal was starting to break off. He bent it back, revealing that underneath was a beating red round tissue. Holding the bloody flesh over it, he twisted it right and wrung it out like a wet rag. The blood dripped directly into the demon's heart, and it beat faster and louder. The machine shook so hard that it caused a small earthquake.

"I think we better go now," Katherine said.

The cult was all around the death machine now. They were breathing in its toxic smoke, drawing in its power. One of them seemed to sense the presence of others and whipped their skeletal head toward the group.

"Now!" Sierra repeated. "They know we're here!"

The cult members were all looking at them now. Their blank expressions were uncaring. The mortals no longer posed a threat to them. One of them even took the time to smile and wave before growing blurry and distant.

The feeling of weightlessness returned to Justin. This time it was the feeling of being grabbed and pulled back by two giant hands. It gave his body a jolt, and he was slungshot backward. This was the complete opposite of the relaxing and tranquil feeling he had going into this dream state. He was full of danger and panic.

CHAPTER FOURTEEN

Justin felt little relief waking back up in the physical world. His back was stiff from laying on the concrete floor, and after struggling to get up, he realized he was the first of three to snap out of the nightmare world. Sierra and Angus laid still. He looked to where Katherine lay. It was empty, and so was the spot where Danielle was.

"Hey, where did you two go?" Justin asked out loud.

He listened for sounds close enough to confirm that the girls were still close by. After two minutes of silence, there was a beeping sound. It came from the camera that was set up to record the ritual. He hoped that it recorded long enough to show what happened to them.

"Ok, let's not do that again," Angus said.

He was now up and no longer trying to hide the fact that he was freaking out.

"Oh no, we didn't all come out at the same time! Where are Danielle and Katherine?" Sierra asked. Her voice was breathy. "She was supposed to pull us all out at the same time," she added.

"We don't know, but hopefully, we can find out by looking at that," Justin answered, pointing at the device's blinking red light.

Sierra examined the camera, pointing out the one dirty fingerprint that was on the record button. She pressed the button to power it back on and went to the beginning of the footage. They could see themselves on the screen lying in the circle, slowly going into a deep trance. They watched their breaths getting slower with each passing minute and eventually stopped altogether.

"Jesus, we look comatose," Angus commented.

"How long do you think we were in that deep?" Justin asked

"I don't know," Sierra said. "Let's skip forward a little bit."

Her finger was shaking when she pressed the screen to move the time frame up, stopping when Katherine started convulsing.

"Oh no, please no." She said.

In the video, Katherine sat up in one robotic-like motion. Her head moved from person to person like someone was controlling her remotely. A vicious smile then spread across her face as she stood up and walked over to the shattered stained glass window. She picked up one long, jagged piece. It was bright blue and resembled a lightning bolt that glowed when the candlelight bounced off of it. Even on the small screen, it was obvious. It was like she hand-picked it just to send a message to its audience.

"Watch this; you're not going to believe what's about to happen."

Katherine circled them with her makeshift weapon in a sick game of duck, duck, goose. It was no mystery as to who the goose was, but when she stopped at Danielle, they were not ready to witness the sadistic act of Katherine raising the sharp glass above her head and thrusting it down into Danielle's chest. Each time it went on deeper and came out stained with a darker shade of red. Danielle squirmed and kicked Katherine and put her hand over her mouth so she couldn't scream and break the other's trance, wiping Danielle's blood on her own shirt.

"Something else took control of her before she could fight back," Sierra said. "That's not Katherine anymore."

A tear rolled down her cheek. It appeared she had just lost

her two friends in two different ways. On the screen, Katherine continued stabbing Danielle over and over. She went deeper and lower each time until she reached her victim's abdomen. Danielle wasn't dead. She still moved but was incapacitated from her injuries. Katherine took her by the feet and dragged her to where the salt barrier still gave them a boundary and used the bloody Danielle as a mop to clear the entire protected perimeter, going off-screen and circling back around until she was in frame again. The poor girl wanted to scream as the white crystals stuck to her open wounds.

Watching this made them feel nauseous. Whatever was controlling Katherine was very amused with itself. It laughed wildly, then turned and looked at the others directly through the camera. She went close to the lens and made sure they could see and hear her perfectly, even performing a fake makeup check to make sure her face looked good.

"Thanks for the vessel," The Katherine thing said. "You know, the salt was kind of unnecessary, we hadn't desecrated the chapel enough yet, and we don't like coming up here unless we have to, but now that your precious little circles are broken, I'm gonna go feed the master a better meal than the last one you gave him. I'll be back for the rest of you. So you guys sit tight until then, ok?"

Evil Katherine then blew a kiss at them and shut the video feed off.

Sierra was baffled.

"It wasn't supposed to go down like this." She said, "she was supposed to be safe. I let her down. I let Danielle down. I'm a fucking failure."

She put her face in her hands and sobbed uncontrollably. Angus tried to put an arm around her, and she rejected it. Justin looked at where Katherine's blood was smeared, where the salt circle used to be. He tried to find even a tiny glimmer of hope in the situation.

"Ok, let's think here; we aren't done yet. I feel like we still need to fight." Angus said.

"What did you have in mind?" Justin asked

"You saw what I saw in there. That damn thing down there has a soft spot. That means it has a vulnerability." Angus pointed out.

"Yeah, but Katherine is possessed; she'll be down there guarding it. She was like my sister, and I'm not an exorcist. I don't know how to undo that without killing her. I just know I can't do it." Sierra said in between sobs.

"You can. I've seen you do some amazing things tonight. Let's find a way to get out of here alive. What if you distract her while I stab the demon right in the heart?" Angus asked.

A cold silence filled the room. Justin did agree with Angus. He, too, saw the demon's soft spot, and if they could convince Sierra to distract Katherine just long enough to give them the advantage, he believed that Angus could take it out. It was their only hope to fight. All they had to do was get Sierra on their side.

"I believe in you too. Even though we just met, you've had the right idea about what needs to be done the whole time. So let's finish this. Let's cleanse this place. Just tell us what to do, and we're with you."

Sierra considered the both of them for a good while. The tears were already drying on her cheeks, and then she took a deep breath and straightened herself out. Her leadership was reestablished.

"If we are going to stand a chance, we can't go down there without protection this time." She told them.

CHAPTER FIFTEEN

"She made sure to clean out all of my good stuff," Sierra said.

The contents of her bag were laid out. There were crystals of various colors, shapes, and sizes. One was long and came to a point like an icicle.

"Those are just precautionary; I have never seen any real results from using them." She told Angus when she saw him pick one up, examining its rough edges and poking the end with his finger.

"Yeah, but it could be used to jab into that thing's weak spot when its energy is focused on controlling Katherine. How do you charge these up?"

"You have to be extremely clear-minded and full of confidence, it absorbs any energy the person holding it out, so you'd have to give it everything you've got. Maybe that's why it never worked for me. Despite the way I come off,' She hesitated," I've never been one hundred percent sure about anything."

He put the crystal in his pocket while just picking up a strange-looking candle; it had some words carved into it. The exact words that Sierra and Katherine had chanted earlier when trying to expel the evil spirits from the incinerator.

"Was this supposed to be used in the ceremony you guys did when we first got here?" Justin asked.

"It was. Danielle must have given me the wrong candle earlier, but it's too late now. Lighting that now won't even put a dent in its energy." Sierra said.

She paused, thinking of an idea so good that she added a finger snap to it.

"However, that might work on the part of it that's controlling Katherine's body. You light that and read it out loud. Then…"

She showed them a small, round, golden mirror that was attached to a necklace.

"If we can trick it into showing us its true form through Katherine, I can make it look at its reflection. If evil reflects upon itself, it will die; after that, you can make your move and stab it in its soft spot," she told Angus.

"How confident do you feel about that plan?" He asked her.

"I'll be honest, after watching three people die tonight, I can't tell you a damn thing about how any of this works anymore, but I just want to say that I'm sorry if we lose. I've never gone up against anything this powerful. Personally, if it cost me my life to stop this thing from taking out this whole town, well, then I say that's worth it. I hope you two feel the same. Even though you had to try not to laugh at us for trying to tell you about this place from the beginning. "

Justin and Angus looked at each other, and Justin could tell by the look in his friend's eyes that he was about to admit to something. He always had that look when he was withholding information ever since they were kids.

"I'm fine with that," he said, not taking his eyes off of Justin's. "Speaking of saving this town, though, I think you should know that you never had to stay for me. I would have made you get out of here and even helped pack and drive you to the bus station. You didn't even realize that I saw your search history over your shoulder the last time we hung out. I saw you look up ticket prices to get a bus to the West Coast. I just thought you'd tell me sooner and wouldn't have second thoughts. That's why I brought you here with me, to show you that I'll be ok now that I had all this going for me."

Angus gestured to everything around them. Justin couldn't help but laugh.

"Yeah, I'd say this is the most effort that I've ever seen you put into anything. What are you gonna do if this works?" He asked.

"Back to living out my hobo living in a van dream. I'll continue to look after this place and make sure groups of idiots don't get themselves trapped in here with fire demons."

"Sounds good," Justin said.

Sierra interrupted their moment of revelation by saying, "ok, so do we need to go over the plan again?"

"Nah," Angus told her. "Light candle, get the demon controlling your friend to look in the mirror at its reflection. Stab the oven demon's heart. Get the fuck out of here. Never speak of anything that happened tonight again. We got it."

"Yeah, and watch our backs; we don't know what kinds of tricks this thing has up its sleeve," Justin added.

"Very good, and since we are coming clean about everything, I have something to add."

Sierra looked away from them, down at the ground, her emotional veil pulled back, and her features softened.

"Before people knew me from the internet, I never bought into the whole demon thing one hundred percent. I was kind of, um, a skeptic."

Both Justin and Angus widened their eyes in disbelief.

"I know," she continued. "Truth be told, I did it to get closer to Katherine. I heard her talking about it around campus one day, and I couldn't help it. Everything about her pulled me in like a magnet, and I wanted to know her better. So I told her I was interested in spirits and demonology. Then when we started hanging out more and talking more about it, I saw how passionate she was. She made me believe in things and see things I never noticed before about the reality we live in, about myself. It helped me gain so much self-confidence, and that's why I'm so protective of her. She's the sister I never had. If I can save her, I'm going to. No matter what happens to me. So if things go south, keep going through with the plan, and if you pull it off, just don't forget us. For a group of dudes that aren't too bright, you're alright," She said, smiling.

"Well, alright then." Justin said, "let's go kill us a demon."

He didn't say anything else, but in Justin's mind, he knew then that he felt more alive than he had in days, maybe even months. He wondered that if all this came to light now, was this life's way of giving him direction? Was he still supposed to just kill a demon and go west pretending that it never happened? How do you start over after something like this? All he knew was that he was saving this town from going down in flames. Then afterward, what if another town needed saving? It was something to consider.

CHAPTER SIXTEEN

A nauseating odor invaded their nostrils. At first, it was like rotten fruit, overcooked meat, and burning charcoal all mixed together. The room was lit with glowing red light, and the walls were the texture of raw meat. The furnace was lit again, once again showing them what the hell's boiler room would look and feel like. The newly possessed Katherine was nowhere in sight, but there weren't too many places she could have gone. There were, in fact, three dark rooms. Coincidentally, one room for each of them to check.

"Ok," Sierra whispered. "If we each take one of these small rooms, one of us will find her and corner her. Yell for me, and I'll keep her busy while you two do the rest. You'll know when I've gotten the demon to see its reflection, trust me."

They split off into the three dark corners where the mysterious rooms waited for them. Sierra used the light from the spell candle, Justin had another candle that was in a glass jar, and Angus had enough light from the ignited incinerator to see into the office. The shells of former filing cabinets and a broken desk were all that remained of the former business setup. They were startled by Angus immediately letting out a sharp yelping sound and then saying, "Damn, there's clothes in here. They're Danielle's. No ghouls, though."

Justin felt his heart race up into his throat and try to pound its way out. The candlelight revealed his room to be a storage place for unfinished tombstones. The names etched in them had either faded out after years of neglect or not been claimed by anyone at all. Leaving Justin to wonder how many people here were buried nameless, possibly with two or three "roommates." If they failed, they would be joining the crowd. Their six faces would be on missing posters being ignored all around town.

Something moved in the shadows, and there was a clank where stone met concrete. The object grew louder and louder as it rolled towards Justin's feet. At first, it was just around the shadow, but as it grew closer, the candle's flame revealed the head of a curly-haired angel statue. He backed away from its grey, blank stare and felt a warm and heavy breath on the back of his neck. It scattered away before he could glimpse it, and he thought about running, but if it was Katherine, he had to keep her in place and call for Sierra.

The headless statue sat in the corner of the room with its arms outstretched. That was the direction the thing that breathed on him had gone, and Justin stepped forward quietly. One of his gifts had always been being light on his feet. He tried to listen for any kind of movement. He formed the plan in his head to sneak up and push the statue down on the figure before it could move again. If it were Katherine, he would have her trapped and stop her from attacking them while Sierra extracted the demon from her. He was pretty sure he could see something behind the decapitated saint holding deathly still.

It hadn't seen him before. He put one hand on one of the cold hard wings and quickly pushed it backward. It tipped with more ease than he was ready for, and the thing let out a small screech as it came down on it. Two arms wriggled out from underneath; if they were Katherine's, something was extremely off about her anatomy. They were shorter and more stubby-looking. The skin was burned to a crisp. As they rubbed together, the black flakes fell off into a pile on the ground until all that was left was bone covered by a thin layer of greasy red muscle.

"Sierra!" Justin meant to cry out, but it came out low and raspy. He realized that whatever it was had no legs; the arms were in their place. "Fuck!" He thought. A trail of goo led to the wall, and he followed it just in time to see a little creature that resembled what was left of Danielle. She was only a torso with arms detached from the shoulders and hanging down loose below her naked chest. She opened her dead mouth and screeched at him before escaping from under the statue. Using the tiny clawed edges on her fingers to scale the wall, dragging the intestines hanging down from her severed belly along.

Then she disappeared into the shadows above him. Justin knew that he couldn't move it in any direction without her having an advantage.

"Angus, SierrA, we have company over here!"

He was able to yell louder this time, but it was already too late. He heard scratching from directly above him, and before he could avoid it, the demon dropped down onto his back. Her teeth were razor-sharp and sunk far down into his left shoulder. He tried turning around and slamming his back against the wall, but the little monster was too fast. She pulled herself upward, causing Justin to keep hitting his shoulder blade against the hard surface. Each time was a sharp pain almost as bad as the bites from her dagger teeth. Then he was being choked. She had managed to get a thick rope of her hair around his neck and was pulling with all her might.

His vision was going blurry, but across the room, he could see another headstone with a statue on top. It was of a colonial-era soldier leading his men into battle. In his right hand was a perfectly sculpted sword; Justin dropped the candle and let it fall to the ground in order to use both hands, he reached back and grabbed evil Danielle, and as hard as he could, he flung her forward. The marble sword went straight through her chest, but she still lived. She shrieked and howled, trying to pull herself off. That's when Angus rushed in, wielding Danielle's discarded salt-covered shirt in his hand. He threw it over her, and her shape disappeared under the cloth until it had completely dissolved.

"What the hell was that?" Angus asked.

"Half of Danielle that was still alive," Justin said, "but it felt like another trap."

Then they heard Sierra scream, and they knew that it wasn't exactly a trap so much as it was just a distraction.

CHAPTER SEVENTEEN

Sierra found Katherine; there were two patches of burned flesh around her eyes. Her strength increased with the extra help of the entity inside her and allowed her to pick Sierra up off the ground by her neck. Her long dirty nails dug in so far that, if she had put any more pressure, they would puncture through the girl's beautiful brown skin. Sierra's eyes, even filled with pain, looked over at Angus and Justin to let them know to stick to the plan no matter what.

"Did you like my pet?" Katherine asked the two but not taking her eyes off of Her victim. When she didn't get a response, she kept taunting them.

"You wanna know how I made her like that? I made that little mortal bitch Danielle submit her body to me before I roasted her. I held her down while the shadow demons took turns entering her mind, leaving part of themselves embedded in her before they tore her in half. You should have seen her in her last moments. She was covered in her own blood, screaming for mercy. You'd think she would know from all the time she spent with us that she'd know the dark ones have no mercy."

Now she turned to them, keeping her grip on Sierra to show that she still had the upper hand.

"But then again, neither do you, huh? You killed my precious little creation, didn't you? Now I guess I'll have to take it out on you, and that's too bad. I can tell this host liked you, Sierra, more than just as a friend. She felt you two were family bound not by blood but in spirit."

With her other hand, she produced the piece of broken stained glass with the dried blood stains painted on it and put it up to Sierra's jugular.

"Say goodbye, darling." She said.

Tears of pain began to form in Sierra's eyes, and Katherine licked them off of her face as they fell.

"Why wouldn't you let her live?" Justin asked, trying to buy them some time. "You could keep her around a link between your world in this one. We know that you can't leave this place. You are trapped here until you've fed that thing enough sacrifices."

He pointed at the furnace and swore that it was moving just like he'd seen it do in the spirit realm. It was the most unsettling part of the experience for him. Now Justin felt that it was acknowledging the fact that he was talking about it. Maybe it was just the heat waves, but had it turned in his direction? Katherine smiled like a lizard who had stumbled upon a whole group of insects to devour.

"You're right about that. We can't leave, and neither can you. You'll die here, and the smoke from your burning bodies will cover everything, the whole town in darkness. That's when everyone will know it's over. This town will become a death trap, and it will start with you. Can't you feel its power growing? You see, we don't need to leave this place. By the time this is over, every person will be drawn to us. They will beg us to sacrifice themselves to the fire."

Katherine was doing precisely what he wanted her to. While she was delivering her speech, Sierra was able to take her mirror on the silver chain out of her pocket. She flipped it open and glanced over with a look in her eyes that said for them to get her attention back towards her.

"I think you need to take a good long look at yourself. You think you're more powerful than her?" Angus said, nodding toward Sierra. "I think she's got your number. I mean, she knows her shit."

Katherine's mischievous grin turned upside down into an elongated scowl. A bit of greenish-yellow drool dripped down from the corner of her bottom lip, and she sucked it back up before it hit the ground.

" You may be the last ones alive, but don't think of yourselves as clever. You've only prolonged the inevitable. Consider this your last sunrise. By the time the next one arrives, all you'll know is darkness; all you'll smell is the sour stench of your rot. She holds no more power than any mortal. Now watch her die."

Katherine drew the sharp glass back for the kill, only to meet her reflection when she faced Sierra's direction. At that moment, no one else could see her reflection, her true form. All they saw was Katherine's skin become transparent. Underneath, a light showed through. Then a dark red light flowed from her like liquid being emptied from a bottle. It exited out of Katherine's mouth and into the mirror. As it drained out, it left her formerly milky white skin a sickly green color. When it was finally over, Sierra clasped the mirror shut. The firm grip that the hand on her throat loosened up, and both women fell to the floor.

Katherine's eyes rolled back in her head. They couldn't see if they were normal again, but even if they could, her stillness would leave anyone to assume they would have no life left in them. Her chest was not moving up and down with the motion of breathing. Sierra sat up and immediately began to sob. The demon was gone, but it took Katherine's soul with it.

"No," she said softly. She took her dead sister's hand and placed it on her wet cheek. Looking for something, anything, to give her hope. There was nothing. Justin and Angus stood there, not knowing what to say. Justin felt defeated; even though they stopped Sierra from getting killed, how would she be ok when they walked out alive? She would never be herself again. He wondered if they should try to comfort her enough to get her to check the door with them and see if they could open it now. Maybe, he thought, they should give her just a few more minutes to grieve her loss.

It had to be almost dawn now, and whatever power held them here would be at its weakest point. They had to have hurt it, there was a piece of it in the mirror now, and they had to destroy it while there was still time. Then Angus uttered the last words they wanted to hear.

"Uh oh," he said.

He was looking at the mirror, and it was jumping across the floor on its own. It found its way into the still-burning fire of the furnace.

CHAPTER EIGHTEEN

"Stab the heart!" Sierra yelled to Angus. Her sadness turned quickly to panic. The soul trapped in the mirror was still a soul that would fuel the evil presence, and if they didn't act soon, they wouldn't stand a fighting chance. The distraction of Katherine's death had made them unfocused, but Angus took his crystal knife out of his belt and charged at the machine. He lifted the flimsy piece of metal, he jabbed at it, and they saw waves of electricity surge through the wires and freeze Angus in place as he was electrocuted.

"No!" Justin shouted.

He was charging forward now, and fire blew from inside the furnace in a great ball. It was cutting off his path. Through the heat waves, Justin saw the front of the furnace twist and contort into a face; its expression was unphased, creating the feeling that it knew what they were going to do. It was one step ahead of them the entire time, moving them like chess pieces. Now everything was still falling into place. Another burst of fire sent Justin flying backward. Pieces of ash rained down from the smoke, along with fragments of bones. Fragments of skulls that never finished burning spewed forth landed around him.

"I can't see through the smoke!" he heard Sierra say.

"We have to get to Angus," he said back.

He got up and forced himself to move through the thick,

suffocating, charcoal-scented air. He saw a silhouette appear ahead of him, tall and hooded, just like the cult members from their quest through the underworld that they were taken on earlier. Not knowing if you could run through a ghost, he fearlessly tried to anyway. When they connected, he realized that it was a solid person.

"Ouch!" Sierra said.

"My fault," Justin apologized

Then the smoke cleared, and there was Angus, dazed but still trying to stab the machine with weak hands, barely holding on to the crystal, which was useless, having not been charged with energy.

"I need to figure out how to get its attention back on me," Sierra thought out loud. She kicked it in the spot where the side of its head would be if it had been a person. When she did this, he saw it become a living thing. In the opening where the fire burned a bright yellow, the shape of a mouth formed. The smaller, red-colored fire that made up the teeth opened and snarled at Sierra. The inner flame formed an oval-shaped cavity. Two metal panels opened up from its side, and two long tentacles made of slippery-looking tissue emerged. They stretched out so long that they could have touched either side of the room. The demon had a complete form now, and it was pissed off.

One of the tentacles reached where Katherine's body lay. It wrapped around her leg and pulled her towards its open mouth.

"No!" Sierra said.

She tried to grab her friend, but it was too late. They watched helplessly as the medium was tossed right into the open mouth of the fire. Sierra screamed out of shock, anger, and fear all the same time. Justin looked to where Angus was still passed out, the crystal in his hand.

"Keep it busy." He said to Sierra. "I'm going for it."

Sierra said nothing. She just looked at the demon straight on, then at the candle with the incantation carved into the side of it, still burning on the floor. Her eyes were two hyper-focus laser beams aimed at the evil, and she repeated the same ritual she and Katherine had tried to perform earlier.

"Evil spirits, standing tall,

It's the time you've made your greatest fall,

We banish you with all our might,

Return to hell thou evil plight,

Go away and leave my sight,

And take with you this endless night."

Her voice sounded powerful, like a sorceress at the peak of her power. A tentacle took a swipe at her, and she dodged it. Meanwhile, the atmosphere in the room began to change. As Justin crawled on the ground to avoid the monster's limbs, he could see the concrete walls harden and turn the color of burned meat with the smell to match. The floor turned smooth and slippery from the tentacles. He felt like he was crawling around the inside of a giant's mouth. The crystal was just out of his reach when one of the tentacles grabbed him. The other one had Sierra. They both were being pulled towards their demise, right into the creature's mouth. Sierra continued chanting her spell, and every few seconds, they felt the grip slightly loosen, but it wasn't enough.

Everything was falling apart at the last minute. They had come so close to saving themselves and the town, too. Justin felt anger and disappointment with himself. He saw his life play out in his mind. In his younger years, before his dad left Justin and his mom because he couldn't accept her deteriorating mental health. His dad let her get carted off to a psychiatric facility down in Florida and just gave up on life. Justin never wanted to be like him. He wasn't a quitter; he didn't want to do what was easy anymore. He needed more time on earth to fix everything he gave up on, especially himself. Something else also occurred to him at that moment.

Shouldn't he be falling into an endless dark abyss right now? That's when he realized the tentacle that had ahold of him had been severed. Angus was back up and had cut him down, and now he was going for Sierra! The crystal knife he had made fun of earlier seemed to glisten like a magic light in his hand as it cut through the tissue of the monster's ligament. The clear, thick fluid that had a musty, earthy aroma came pouring out of it, and if Justin wasn't mistaken, he heard the thing howl.

"I did it!" Angus declared. "I got you fucker!"

The monster let out another guttural howl. Sierra repeated her spell, louder with each verse, and it was working. The wounds from the crystal had weakened it. Just when all hope seemed lost, they were going to see the light of another day after all.

CHAPTER NINETEEN

A strong wind came out of the inside of the beast's mouth, sucking inward instead of blowing out. The interior of the flame began spinning around, pulling everything towards it with the force of a growing tornado. Even though it was dying, it was going to take everything with it. All of the rot and ash and the tombstones were sucked into the hateful vortex. The whole world folded in on itself. Angus pointed out the only thing that wasn't in danger of being pulled in was because it was bolted to the ground.

"Over there!" He said, pulling at Justin's arm. He was guiding him towards the second furnace; the older one was the best spot to take shelter. Their feet slid as they struggled to get across the floor.

"What about Sierra?" Justin asked.

"We'll all fit," Angus said. He grabbed her by the arm too. She was still using the banishing spell even after it worked, and her power stance made it harder to move her out of place.

"Come on!" Angus urged her.

She finally let herself be led toward the cover of the other machine that wasn't inhibited by a living evil being. She was ushered in by Angus first, then Justin. Then it was slammed shut. Leaving him in the darkness, just like the one he was in before Angus woke him up out of his drunken nap. Justin pounded on the small metal door with his foot.

"Angus, get in here with us! What are you doing!."

There was a brief pause from the other side, then Angus spoke softly, calmly.

"Yeah, listen, about that. Aside from getting electrocuted earlier, that thing got me pretty good before I stabbed it. You couldn't see it, but the fucker cut me up, and I'm bleeding out, Justin. I don't think I have too many minutes left, and you know what? I'm ok with this. I've always planned on dying here. There's nothing left outside of this place for me, but there is for the both of you. So do me a favor and just let me have this; stay in there until this is over with. Cool?"

Justin felt a knot form in his chest. How did not notice that Angus was wounded? Couldn't they still save him? He wanted to argue that they could, but in the back of his mind, he knew it was useless. Angus was so stubborn. He was always the one who wanted to hang on to the life he's always had. He was the only thing that stayed consistently good about the town that Justin was so desperate to get out of for good.

"Remember what I said, Justin. Don't let this place hold you back."

He said that like he could read Justin's mind.

"I'm sorry I wasn't a better friend." That was all Justin could think to say.

"You were an excellent friend, and you know it."

Then, there was nothing but the sound of the howling wind pulling in everything in its path, giving way to absolute silence. The world was still again. Angus was gone now, too. Justin could feel it.

"You think it's safe to go out there?"

He asked Sierra solemnly. He couldn't see her, but he pictured her looking so tired. Her energy had to have been completely drained from finally completing her first banishing spell. Her eyes were probably heavy and tear-stained. He could hear her sniffle in between saying. "I think so." Then Justin let his emotions go, and he cried too. They stayed there for a while, embracing each other in the darkness.

When they came out, there was a stream of daylight coming from the open bay door. Where it shined was the space where the incinerator stood. Now it was just a blank space. After all, they had been through; they approached the rising sun with caution. It was hard to be sure if it was real or if they, too, had died. That would mean the light would lead them to the other side, whatever that was anymore. He felt Sierra's hand slip into his. It was cold, but after spending the night in what felt like the bowels of hell, the cold was good. They proceeded back to the outside world, a sight that made one night feel like a decade had passed.

The sidewalk was filled with early risers, joggers, and people just getting home from a long night of partying. That made Justin think of Trent. The jerk was probably passed out now. He would leave him a note and not even have to speak to him about moving out if he hurried. Sierra stood in the cemetery, looking at the headstones covered in overgrown weeds and the dead trees.

"Well, looks like your work here is done," he told her.

"It's not." She said back. "This place was never right. The poor souls here, buried on top of each other. What happened last night can never happen again. Someone has to stay and look over this place. Think it still needs a good caretaker?"

"Yeah." He told her, "You'd be perfect for that."

She smiled sadly at him.

"What do we tell people?" He asked.

"I think no matter what we say, they'll just think we're crazy."

He agreed with that. He wondered, though, if anyone could have heard their screams or if there was black smoke coming out of the smokestack as the furnace burning. No one called the police about trespassing, so maybe no one had ever seen or heard anything. Sierra would have to answer for Katherine and Danielle's disappearance. Justin didn't know Neil well enough, but it made him sad all over again, knowing that no one was left to even wonder where Angus was and if he was ever coming back. All that was left of him was his van.

That van was going with Justin. He was leaving and continuing the journey Angus never took in it. West it was. He was going to study video game design and take Angus with him in spirit everywhere he visited along the way. He just hoped that the keys were still in the same hiding place as always.

"Hey, I'm glad we met. In the end, you and Angus saved everyone's ass back there." He told her as they parted. "I'm sorry you lost your sister."

"I'm sorry you lost your best friend." She said back. Then he left her there and went to the van, where sure enough, the keys were under the front bumper. Angus never believed in keeping them very well hidden; after all, he was never very far from his home. The driver's seat felt like it was still warm like no one ever left it.

CHAPTER TWENTY

It didn't take long to load the last of his belongings into the spacious vehicle. When it came down to it, there wasn't much he owned. Some clothes, his prized baseball bat, his Playstation 5, that one he rarely got to use. Every time he went to the living room to play it, there would sit Trent and his goons. They were always on it playing shoot 'em up games online. Justin had never had any interest in senseless garbage like that. He liked games that took strategy to beat. Speaking of Trent, he was sitting on the porch, watching Justin load his things and smoking out of his ugly brown pipe that Justin hated.

He must have found the note that was left for him. It wasn't very long after all. It simply read:

Dear Trent, I'm moving out to go travel; here's my cut for this month's rent, good luck.

That was it, and Trent was not bothered by it. He only gave a simple nod when Justin gave one last glance at him before shutting the back doors of the vehicle. The morning sun bounced off of something and created a beam of bright light that reflected off the metal surfaces. After shielding his eyes, Justin spotted an old container that Angus had kept since they were teenagers.

It was his officially licensed Spellbinder and The Warriors of Time lunch box. The front of the aluminum box depicted wizards engaging in an epic battle. In the background, four wizards each stood high on top of a mountain, commanding different mythological creatures to do battle. Each creature was the color that corresponded with its master's robe. They were tethered to their master by beams of light coming from the wizard's hands. Forming puppet strings that hovered over the dragons, falcons, giants, and cyclops. Justin always loved that box. He was one of the few who got to see the geeky side of Angus that got excited about fantasy card games. He wondered if it still held the unique treasure he thought it did.

He flipped the latches, and sure enough, there they were, still in perfect condition. All the cards in the series lay in perfect stacks in the order that Angus always played them in. Justin went to the back left pile and reached for the one on the very bottom, the one that was still in a clear plastic case. One in ten of the series came with the golden orb card. Justin remembered being there the day Angus opened it in the comic book store, where they spent a lot of their time looking at all the collectibles.

The golden orb card was notable in that if you held it up to the light, a message would appear in the orb that only the player using it could see. It would guide you by telling you which of your elemental cards to put together to cast the best spell. Angus would always win by breaking out that card, and he would never let it go. Even after their years of playing role-playing fantasy card games were over.

Justin smiled, and another lone tear rolled down his cheek. If they only knew that those carefree days would be their best memories together.

He took the card out and held it up to the sunlight, then cupped his hand to it to see if it still worked, and his heart stopped.

"HEY, ASSHOLE, WHO TOLD YOU IT WAS OK TO TOUCH MY RARE CARD?"

He blinked to make sure he wasn't seeing things, but the message in the orb was still there.

"No fucking way," he said out loud. He wondered if Trent could see him, but he had gone inside.

"Out of all the things, you're gonna possess a card game?"

The message in the orb disappeared. Justin frantically rubbed his eyes to eliminate the possibility of fatigue-induced hallucination, then did the same process of holding it up to the sun. This time when he cupped his hand over the card, it read:

"YOU GOT A PROBLEM WITH THAT?"

Justin laughed. He couldn't believe it; his friend was coming with him, after all, in a way.

"No, this is cool. I just wanted you to know that I'll take good care of your van house. I promise I won't wreck it, and I'll find odd jobs to make money for gas until I get to where I'm going. I'm glad I can still talk to you, you know, from the other side and all that."

He checked for a new message. This time it said, "DON'T MAKE IT WEIRD, JUST DRIVE." So he put the card back in its plastic case and into his jacket pocket. He would guard that with his life. Of course, it would be worth mentioning to Sierra too. Before leaving her, he did promise himself that he would visit her sometime and see how she was doing with her new demon extracting and cemetery caretaker business. Most people would write her off as a hoax, another person trying to draw attention to her money-making scheme, but Justin had seen what she could do. He would be one person who would never doubt her. Hell, maybe when the time was right, he would see if she needed his assistance on any of her more complex cases.

For now, he needed to get going. He started the vehicle, and it roared to life like it was brand new. He decided to take the old route to the interstate that their school bus did. He and Angus would flip off all the trendy places that started to replace the old small businesses in town. He thought it would be fun to do that. He was nervous but excited. This is where life truly started for him, and he would never lose sight of who he was again. He finally had an idea of how he wanted to spend the rest of his life.

As for his friend, his life was cut short but not over. There was no end, only another journey for him. However, this town, the place they hung onto was the end of a chapter. Its changes couldn't be undone, and his old life with it. That was the actual death, the death of the past. It died with Angus' physical body, but his spirit moved on to a new town, and Justin couldn't wait to ask him about it.